Heroes Are Grazing
in My Garden

Heberto Padilla

HEROES ARE GRAZING IN MY GARDEN

Translated from the Spanish by
ANDREW HURLEY

Farrar · Straus · Giroux

NEW YORK

Library of Congress Cataloging in Publication Data
Padilla, Heberto.
Heroes are grazing in my garden.
Translation of: En mi jardín pastan los héroes.
I. Title.
PQ7390.P3E513   1984   863   83-20686

Translator's Note

I should like to express my sincerest thanks to Heberto Padilla for his kindness, patience, understanding, and help in preparing this English version of his novel. For her help in the checking and correction of the manuscript, I am grateful to Aileene Alvarez; and for that aid and more besides, to my wife Isabel Garayta.

—*Andrew Hurley*

Part One

THE SAME SUITCASE she had carried on all her trips (indestructible leather and straps)—Gregorio Suárez took it down tenderly from the top of the closet and Gloria and his mother-in-law cleaned it till it gleamed. The baby watched them from the crib, bouncing up and down.

"He wants to take a trip too," his mother-in-law said.

The brightness of a splendid day came in through the window. It was now seven o'clock in the morning and his mother-in-law placed everything she would need for the trip in the bag. She sighed endlessly and repeated over and over how much she'd miss them, but she never left the dresser mirror, where again and again she nervously stroked and patted her hair. Gloria appeared with two cups of coffee, which they began slowly to drink. Gregorio went to his study, and when he was sure neither of the women could see him, he pulled away the hidden board behind one of the shelves and took out the dark brown, shiny, clothbound diary that he had kept for ten years and regularly wrote in. He hurriedly noted: "Only a few hours to go."

He returned the diary to its hiding place and took out

[3]

the bottle of rum from behind the volumes of the encyclopedia. That was the first drink of the day. Then would come the others, one after another. He rinsed out his mouth. "I'm going to do something about this tomorrow if it kills me." His room was frightfully clean and neat. The typewriter was on the table, immaculate. Gloria's work—her stubborn, persevering work.

From the nearby buildings he began to hear the talk as the students who were getting ready to go to their classes jumped out of their bunks, parted their mosquito nets, and made lines for the bathrooms. The great houses of the bourgeois now sheltered this ferocious teenage impatience which destroyed the mahogany balustrades and the great mirrors on the walls, beneath which resided fine porcelain urns. The oil portraits of the old ladies who had occupied the houses were now flanked by propaganda murals, on which the revolutionary government proclaimed its hopes, its strength, and its violence. All that, enormously plastic in his hands. A concrete, eloquent scene, no analysis, no psychology or sociology. Pure description. And dialogue? Direct, no dashes, no quotation marks, no "he said" or "he exclaimed" or "he shouted" or "he whispered." A verbal web, a fabric without unnecessary, merely rhetorical, fissures. No antecedent theory. Blank time.

In the other mansions, still private, almost abandoned, no movement could be discerned. But he was sure behind the shutters the same old stubborn eyes were spying. Get that down, scrutinize and understand every aspect of that life—through representation, not through analysis. Pure evidence. Old Zaida and Fernández Junco like bloodhounds on everyone's track. Julio and Luisa, alone, more or less young. They cordially kept their distance. They smiled when they went out or came in. Don't forget the huge house they lived in—two stories, surrounded by abandoned walled gardens with wrought-iron gates—the tall weeds taking it over, the gigantic vines. Receptions in the past, the many wrought-iron tables, scattered every few feet, rusted now, relics with flaking white enamel. Don't overlook anything. The furtive exits of the couple, the occasional visits by two or three friends, the three lighted rooms and the rest of the great house in darkness. They conversed with Zaida and Fernández Junco; it was a fairly indolent relationship. The old people came to them and not the other way around, frequently spoke to them in lowered voices; they listened with that acquiescence in which cordiality is mere form.

"I think we'll have to find a taxi," said Gloria.

And at that moment Gregorio saw Julio and Luisa driving the little blue Opel toward the Quinta Avenida.

The Opel descended the street behind the hotel, between the playing field and the pool, and turned down the Malecón from Miramar. Rodríguez lost sight of it a little before it turned. Once more, he picked up the photograph from the top of the desk.

"Who brought the report?"

"The Security people," Edmundo said.

"I wish they'd quit fucking around—Julio was sent by ORO. He's supposed to be trustworthy, and it's no secret to anybody here that bureaucrats are filling the whole country with shit. We're not going to throw everybody in jail who makes some comment on something. That man reminds me of somebody. I've seen him somewhere, but I can't quite remember. Have you heard anybody say anything about him, Edmundo?"

He couldn't know him, of course; years had passed, though for the veterans of the movement, since its beginning in 1953 the years had passed like days. '53, '59, '65—it was as though they flowed smoothly one into the next; but Rodríguez had had a heart attack and some of his younger friends had experienced sudden sharp pains. Others had actually died; only Fidel had remained vigorous, healthy, enthusiastic, his face unchanged from year to year. *He* couldn't be counted among the Old Guard; compared to him, even a young man like Edmundo seemed like a bloodless automaton. The Revolution was entering an inevitable period of "definitions." Everyone's heart had stopped when the national press indiscriminately reprinted foreign news reports about the Soviet Union's invasion of Czechoslovakia; three tense days, during which the most dissimilar and contradictory opinions were heard, but only an idiot could expect any other outcome. Fidel had acted in the only possible way—politics was a matter of concrete needs, demands. With pretexts identical to the U.S.S.R.'s in Czechoslovakia, the United States could invade us; but its internal conflicts no longer made that possible, and now the important thing was not to lose Czechoslovakia. It was naïve to expect anything else. However, Rodríguez had lived through those tense hours possessed by a kind of uncontainable exultation. The rebel underlay any logical realist; the old guerrilla enthusiasm still governed him.

Edmundo could know nothing of this; he merely put in order the reports that came in. He typed them up neatly and placed them in the proper folders. What the

State Department of Security turned in was for him the sole truth. The Old Guard considered the *man*, his contradictions and human conflicts. Edmundo simply went by the reports. Every man was only that, a report, with all its natural margin of error, but conjecture and conclusions were the job of the apparatchiks and the Party.

The vague image of Julio disturbed Rodríguez. At some moment in his undercover work he had heard the name. He looked at Edmundo. "Why the hell do you wear those clothes, man?"

"They brought them to me."

"But my God, they're not from here."

"They brought them to me."

"But you could wear them at night, Edmundo. Here you're just conspicuous. We've got a difficult situation in the country, and you know very well where you're working."

Edmundo felt as though Rodríguez had pointed out a blemish to him. That grotesque getup, whatever it might be, wasn't voluntary. Dirty clothes had been piling up in his room over the last two weeks. He no longer had a Gabi to take care of them. Domestic life was now his to deal with as best he could, since he had begun to live the life of a bachelor—or an abandoned husband. Rodríguez took up the photograph again, looked at it carefully. Sometime during the Revolution he had met this man. There was no doubt about it.

"Tell them to stop fucking around. Do you hear me? Humberto recommended him and ORO approved him and they must have his dossier."

The overzealousness of the police in the last few years irritated him—that ferocious scrutiny of every-

[7]

thing that was said in the country. He was the first to admit that a revolution was indeed a serious matter, but a zeal that was merely professional and that set itself up as the only and indisputable moral force alarmed him. Therefore—it couldn't be avoided—the figure of Edmundo repelled him. He was an ally, a militant, but symmetrical, cold, one-sided. What did *this* man know of men?

"I don't want you to feel bad. You're no stranger to the problems that have been cropping up recently. They say all revolutions rot. We have to take care of ours. So it doesn't rot."

Fidel's picture—the beardless face of a twenty-year-old —presided over his office from above. How far away that time had become. It had been a time for kneading history, dominating reality. And this nice boy had a right to that too, this nice young man sitting before him, looking from his own vantage point at the photograph of the man who had made history just as Rodríguez himself had—Julio, from ORO, militant, so the police report stated, brave, now under injunction. He spoke out resentfully, and high positions were withheld from him because of it; he didn't conceal his criticisms. He had been reduced to being a mere interpreter of English, French, and German. But he even criticized the Revolution to those he assisted—the Institute for International Friendship used his services by order of ORO.

Rodríguez couldn't tell if it was a feeling of pity or obscure rejection which he felt toward Edmundo. He denied it, but at the bottom of his heart he had a feeling it was the inevitable rejection of one generation by another. It isn't possible to love a man who hasn't taken part in our struggle, who hasn't been moved by the

[8]

news of a certain historical moment. Edmundo claimed (or showed) an innocence that they challenged and judged. Dopey, talkative Gabi, his wife, in spite of superficial differences, had the same essence. Beneficiary of the perfectly coherent epoch that she was chosen to live in. But he didn't want to humiliate Edmundo. He didn't like to humiliate anyone. The desire to humiliate another person made one somehow less; something frustrated, bitter, unresolved, pricked one to make the severest judgments on others. Being the boss, directing something or someone, having a subordinate at one's side, criticizing him, demanding of him behavior that one didn't exhibit oneself; no. Humiliating him was humiliating oneself.

When he left, when he was once more breathing the natural air of the street, he kept thinking about Edmundo as intensely as he thought of Julio. Such extremes! It was like a game; only years changed the opponent's physiognomy. Under the glaring sun, he thought that youth was like fireworks, a kind of display in which the vital and the ostentatious were inseparable. But the photograph Security had sent him had not been that of a young man. It was a contemporary's face that was disturbing him. How easy to put an informer before an eager mouth, a desperate heart! Did revolutions always, inevitably, have to feed on some disgusting little tidbit of information, be nourished by sentiment or fanatical zeal? Rodríguez knew that he was in the grip of that "mid-life crisis" which made him happy to be mature and despair to be growing old.

When he was almost to the corner of his house, the first thing he noticed was his dog waiting for him—his ears down, his gaze alert, the wagging tail, the barks, the love. But Nazis too, goddamnit, Nazis had loved dogs, had given more love to animals than to people.

Edmundo couldn't contain the sense of freedom he experienced after his conversations with Rodríguez. He sighed and thought of calling Gabi (it was an instinctive reaction); but Gabi no longer waited for his call, and this current crisis, which had all the signs of being the last, certainly did not make him happier than Rodríguez. Rodríguez went back to a home, a wife, a dog; Edmundo wasn't even sure what Gabi's telephone number was— yet he had instinctively been about to call her. And so *his* habits were exactly like those of middle-aged men. He was the prisoner of a body, an odor, a way of life—in short, a habit. He dialed Braulio's number, or rather, Cuca's, the children's, the house's, the home's, whatever —at least, some home's. Braulio hadn't come in yet; neither had Cuca. He heard the older daughter calling from an upstairs bedroom. He said he'd call later. Almost at once his phone rang. It was Arsenio, from Security.

"I don't know what we have to do to convince Rodríguez that that man is resentful, at the least, and a threat to our work. By now he's probably poisoned the Swedish woman with the venom he spews out. We don't want to exaggerate, but Rodríguez has plenty of proof; we've given him all the data." Edmundo agreed indifferently. It was the old battle of duties—one side pledged to a normal, technical vigilance; the other, too deeply burned in the struggle, striving to save men. Or "man," as they said every time they spoke of vigilance, of stiffening the political, revolutionary guard. Behind this, Rodríguez always saw the opportunist. The photograph of Julio, taken right there in the hotel (the thin mature face, the large eyes, impatient or desperate, but somehow out of place), was still on Rodríguez's desk, next to the latest report on his counterrevolutionary opinions. Edmundo could see the hotel pool in the photo, and he could make out the Russian swimmers— the thick, heavy, round, flushed baby faces of country girls. Their companions were drinking between dips in the pool; the girls were talking and seeing to the children, who were playing all around. They drank interminably. The first time he had tried to push himself to drink the way they did, it had left him wasted; he was nauseated for two days, unable to get out of bed, tended by the tolerant Gabi of old. With his eyes bloodshot from too much alcohol, he saw Gabi's trembling image, but over the years it had faded away, obliterated by trunks and airports—the Gabi that little by little had become embittered toward him. The difficulties of the political movement had eaten away like an acid at habits, dreams, even the deepest loyalties. It had all ended up in a deserted bedroom with piles of unwashed clothes, in a bachelor, in the unending chatter of Norma and the parrot Panchón, which fell on him like a blizzard of reproaches. Of course, they all thought Gabi was right. He was indeed a chronic idler. Panchón chattered, heaped slanderous names on him. He'd never amount to anything, he'd spend his whole life in ORO sniffing out the political doubts of his comrades. Nuria, though, was always reserved, distant, when she listened. She looked on him with pity and even tried to be there when her sister and brother-in-law corraled him. She would cross the living room and go and lie down in the farthest bedroom. Strange silent creature. What did she represent in their lives? Probably a severe judge, perhaps even his own judge. Maybe what he thought was pity in her really was distance, indifference, the border that a separate world establishes. But Nuria possessed an attractive, mysterious haughtiness, a self-assurance, which frightened him. He couldn't tell why she reminded him of the girl in Dostoevsky's *Notes from Underground,* a mousy creature in a world she was both part of and not part of, and from which a sudden fire in her eyes freed her. How different were these big husky Russian girls of political export from those girls he had known in Moscow, lovely and badly dressed, Russian girls out of Chekhov and Turgenev, almost misty— cordial but impenetrable! He would watch them pass by in the afternoons, on Gorky Street, as he left the counterintelligence classes he and several others were taking from Party comrades. Since then, when he had been among them, he had never felt so alive, so much a man.

From the Hotel Nacional, Rodríguez always walked home along the same street; if he had been asked why, he couldn't have explained; his route was more a moral position than habit—and in the last few years it was mortally linked, as well, to the Revolution because of the fascination he derived from watching it mature and develop. He smiled at that "mortally" which came to his head; but it was true that he was irremediably tied to this Revolution. Too many things had happened that he had had to make his peace with. A revolution is not simply the excited rush of plans, dreams, old longings

for redemption and social justice that want to see the
light of day which the revolution gushes at its beginning. It has its dark side, too, difficult, dirty almost—
repression, overzealous police vigilance, suspicion, sum-
mary verdicts, firing squads. One had no choice. The
totality included all of that, and he, too, was part of
the totality—perhaps one of those least importantly
responsible?—but part, too. The frequent stabs of pain
on his left side, just before his heart attack, came to his
mind.

It is curious how sight acquires with habit a great
capacity for blindness. The eye adapts rapidly, loses the
memory of things—it hardly took in the deterioration
of the old business signs that rain was flaking off,
blurring, and fading, the storefronts, once sparkling,
today gray and filthy—everything about the look of the
street had changed. Everywhere he saw doors installed
suddenly in old garages that now sheltered the homeless,
old warehouses in disuse, boarded up. All of that created
a new atmosphere. In the course of year after year, he
hardly noticed how things had been radically altered.
But at certain crises in the country, always foreshadowed
by large public meetings in the Plaza de la Revolución,
he would stand and look around, searching for a physical,
external response to the inevitable unrest. His street had
changed. Was it a change toward happiness? Or were
these filthy façades still the larval, primitive state of the
future? He observed once again the line people made in
front of the Volga Restaurant, the flock of people at the
Club 23, the lines they made next to the little shops
that sold cigars and cigarettes, since they had to be
rationed, too. He felt drawn to the shortest of them and
stood in line between a tired bureaucrat and a heavy,

panting woman—he, too, could get two packs of Popu-
lares, which he quickly stuffed into his briefcase. At
least these little daily escapes brought him in touch with
a reality that lay beyond the great mahogany doors of
the Hotel Nacional, where the Party had put him since
his heart attack. Rodríguez loved production more than
anything (he had been acting director of the Ministry
of Industry, in charge of four plants). "But everywhere
one can be useful." It was true. The hotel was a kind of
stage where political and police plotting was acted out,
and he had to protect it. The strange thing was that the
hotel was run more by State Security than by Tourism.
On the street, in the lines, the collective fatigue over-
came him as intensely as the problems that he knew
about and the people didn't.

It wasn't right to think yourself too good to rub elbows
with the people, even though it was uncomfortable to
do it. It wasn't good not to know people's lives; it was
better to walk, see, hear, talk to people in the street.
Many of his friends had become cruel, contemplating
with contempt the situation now general in the country;
the lives of real people seemed less important to them
than the inexactness of economic information, the in-
completeness of a plan, or the lack of efficiency in
economic leadership. But those were sufferings that
Rodríguez thought of as too professional, too restricted
to a specific area; he thought of this zeal which was only
disturbed by totality as a kind of aristocratic distance.

He frequently spoke with his wife about these walks.
She, too, saw what others did not even mention; she was
upset by the same governmental shortcomings he was.
They spoke in allusions, little comments which added
up to a dramatic and pessimistic conclusion and which

they both struggled mightily to dissolve, make disappear. The difficult, hard flank of the movement.

Walking wasn't a bad idea, the doctor had told him; at a certain age, one had to forgo the sedentary life; the old man who lies down perishes. Activity is a characteristic of childhood and a necessity of old age; but this sun, this atmosphere, this humidity that battered him were intolerable. And also a shattering proof that he was growing old.

The dog jumped up and down, sprang at him happily. Rodríguez petted him with his right hand, repeating, "Okay, Cinnamon, okay," trying to calm him down, trying to avoid the effort that could make even sharper the terrifying, frequent pain that pierced his chest. He refused the coffee Angela offered him; he'd rather rest awhile before dinner; he'd had a rough day, full of people. But his wife needed few words to understand that. She tied up the dog.

"Humberto called," she said from the living room.

"Oh? What was it?"

"You'd probably already left the hotel when he called."

Rodríguez could perfectly imagine what it was about, since Humberto was Luisa's brother and Luisa lived with Julio in Julio's enormous rotting house.

"He's coming to see you tonight."

"I have a terrible headache."

"Rest awhile; you know he always comes late."

Obviously, the walk was now too much for his health. The old physical constitution he prided himself on, so few years ago, had called time-out, needed a truce too,

and so did his emotions. How humiliating are the limits
nature imposes on the body! And how late one learns
that lesson! There, lying on the bed, breathing with
difficulty while Angela tried to calm Cinnamon down,
who was whining at the imposition of the chain,
Rodríguez—who had no family but this woman who
hardly spoke, for whom being slender was the major
worry of her life, and this dog—plump, stretched out,
dense, affectionate—had no fear whatever of death. But
he wanted it to come at work, in the street, not in a
wheelchair, not in bed.

In a little while, Angela said, "Security has been driving around here all day."

"What?"

"Apparently a Russian was poisoned somewhere near
here last night."

Rodríguez heard the news with concern.

"Those people'll get into anything," Angela added.
"They've finished off all the 90-proof alcohol, and apparently last night someone gave them wood alcohol to
drink, can you imagine? He was just a kid, a navy officer.
Just imagine, he died right there, poor thing."

That night, when Humberto arrived, he had little to
add to what Rodríguez suspected. Humberto tried to
turn the conversation into an exchange on the understanding of a "case"; but they both knew they were
kidding themselves. Julio was beyond their comprehen-
sion and their help. Julio had been "appointed"; one got
nowhere by insisting. Strange—what stuck most fixedly
in Rodríguez's memory was the first rain of winter,
those rains that came and went like the constant sun

of summer. They were irrational, sudden rains, crazy rains that might cover the country or be no more than two acres across, but rains that couldn't be ignored, a great alluvion of remorseless water.

What did it matter to him, now that Julio was a bureaucrat under injunction!

He knew perfectly how these mechanisms of nullification worked, to favor someone or destroy him. Let them fire him from his job at ORO, not use him anymore as an interpreter, let them do whatever they bloody wanted to!

He understood Humberto, though, the complex fraternal jealousy that brought him here, to Rodríguez; but what could they do against a mechanism greater than they? Rigor, vigilance, political loyalty's demands became decisive forces. None of them could do anything for him. Too much understanding could be taken for weakness.

In the rain, Humberto's great carcass became an anomalous receding shadow, an anomalous shadow that faded into smoke. Rodríguez breathed even more anxiously, with a strong feeling of impotence. His wife watched him serenely; there was a clinical distance in her attitude. Raimundo could add little. He moved nervously about the room, repeated the same arguments as his bosses—Julio was not a man, he was a "case." He had been ordered not to go on seeing the Swedish girl; they told Raimundo that he, rather, should take charge of her, that they should get rid of the resentful Julio as quickly as possible. Raimundo spoke with some agitation, but he said it all. Every word reechoed in that sharp, faint, but growing pain the doctor had pinpointed. Raimundo, too, was lost, faded into smoke, in the violent downpour. Rodríguez's wife observed him with the old understanding that had come with their years together. She said nothing. She tied the dog to its post as it was trying to escape.

Rodríguez listened to the rain beating on the roof and windows. His wife went to the window, drawn by a noise from outside.

"Is something going on?" Rodríguez asked.

His wife had put a chair by the window and was trying to look out.

"There are a lot of people," she said.

"What is it?" he insisted.

"The Russian," she said. "It looks as if they're taking him with them."

"Is he really dead?"

"Well, he's covered with a sheet and they're putting him in the ambulance."

Part Two

GREGORIO slid into the taxi and rode down the avenue bordered with almond and flamboyant trees, feeling a joy so exultant that he imagined himself some gaudy insect. He was not repelled by the comparison. It suggested the virtually larval life he had been living for the last few years, the swarm of moths wheeling around his desk lamp at night, the pages crawling with furiously scratched-out lines, and hidden, so that Gloria couldn't find them; in their lair they coexisted fraternally with the surreptitious fauna that filled the room he worked in, especially at night; but he spoke of that neither to Gloria nor to his two friends—only of symbols, textures, structures, and linguistic fabrics, to be fashionable. He accepted, as they did, that the true protagonist of a novel is language, and he, like his contemporaries, had discovered his language a good while ago—doing parodies. It was a pleasant way to resurrect the great styles, great works. When he was alone, however, he dreamed of Dickens—of his good and evil people, his pity and irony and tenderness, his streets and inns, and of that power that gave his words a strong sudden enchantment. He was convinced—*that* art could never die.

The taxi's unexpected detour (the tunnel on the

avenue was temporarily closed) roused him from his musings. The taxi headed toward the iron bridge and he watched the luminous delta of Almendares come into view, suddenly flowing into the Moskva, into the dirty, murky canal where his stubborn memories glinted, but immediately he jumped to the Habanilla River. Engineers and peasants clustered around the entrance to the channel, the demolition bombs threw up walls of silt and concrete, the great alluvial bank swelled, becoming a huge lake between mountains; the electric plant illuminated the night of Escambray. This was the starting point, the world he needed to internalize, understand— love. Every day he had to win a new battle against those morbid memories—start over. But who asked him to start over, to write again? He really didn't like the world of writers, people who watch one another—their illnesses, quarrels, failures, conjugal squabbles, hidden writings, birth dates. He had suddenly disappeared from that world; he could still open the window and hear the applause that had celebrated the disappearance. Nonetheless, on the table he worked at there was still the notebook with the words *Order of the Day* at the top, and, held with a clip, the sheaf of cheap paper with Gloria's perfect calligraphy: "Today you owe ten pages. December 6."

The taxi left the bridge behind, entered the streets of Vedado, headed toward the Avenue of the Presidents. Beyond the window he saw now, as he had never seen before, the way years had eroded the houses and buildings set about by untamed vegetation. This, this too he must describe, as a point of contrast. He smiled. There on the sills of broken windows balanced an uncontainable future like a child's fire.

This, moreover, was a special day. His mother-in-law was leaving. He looked at the old visage; a leaden rhomboid covered with gray hair, hundreds of wrinkles circling eyes vanquished but still alert. Then he thought of Nuria's face. It wavered; it drew away, approached, drew away again, an adorable sketch whose contours he couldn't quite make out.

His mother-in-law gave a long sigh of fatigue. Nuria's would be a happy, deep breath after the day's work. Her hair, long, black, and ruffled, over her eyes. He'd have to write it all down that very night, the tiny impressions that would give life to his story.

The taxi stopped in front of the train station. He got out first and helped the taxi driver with the bags; then he helped her. He made his way, pushing and shoving as well as he could, through the crowd that pressed against the platform railing—trying to persuade the porter to wait for that heavy, slow mass, one foot dragging after the other, her huge hand shaking her purse as she walked—for he wanted to get her aboard as soon as possible, to get her seated, to hear again the same warnings, the same advice spoken the entire route between the house and the train station, which, fortunately, he would not have to hear during the coming months.

The porter finally gave in, but hurried them along. Lean, sweaty, impatient, almost desperately asking them to move faster. There was no one left on the platform. They were about to give the order to close the gates. The train was going to depart any second. It was smoky in the half light, in the metallic shade, almost spectral. At last they managed to leave behind the bustle and shoving, and climbed into the coach. He put down the bags, helped her to sit down: "Lean on my shoulder." Every-

thing would be all right, don't worry. It wouldn't be the
first time they had had to take care of the boy themselves.
Everybody worked and still managed to arrange things
with their kids.

The sweaty face went on imploring. He placed the
little pillow behind her neck. "It's only fifteen hours.
They'll go by before you know it." He squeezed her
cold hands, kissed her on her spongy cheek. What you
must do is pull yourself together. Everything would be
better when she came back. From the passageway he felt
her eyes still calling to him, following him, trying to
hold him. He went back to hear what she was saying. On
one of the many little windows he saw an arm making a
transparent circle on the dusty glass. Through it Nuria
waved to him, signaling uneasily, urgently, with unchar-
acteristic vehemence. He bent toward the old woman,
listening to that monochord whisper of hers, but still
looking toward the little window, toward the impatient
hand, too impatient and clichéd and conventional and
ridiculous—at once too fictitious and truculent. He cut
it off.

The old woman went on pleading. Gregorio insisted
that he needed absolutely nothing. There was nothing
to worry about. Everything had already been taken care
of. Gloria wasn't a child, she was a mother. Yes, he
understood. He would probably think the same way
when the baby grew up. The old face moved with
emotion for the first time; it even smiled. Nuria smiled,
too, at the end of the passageway, hiding her hands in
embarrassment.

"Have a good rest," Gregorio said, "and write to us."
The old woman waved goodbye. He went off, down the

passage, went toward the door of the carriage, went down the steps, stopped a moment on the platform.

At dusk, with the comforting arrival of night, a breeze would blow from off the mountains, groups of girls would be in the dormitories, the Chinese lantern hung above the immaculate cots, and Nuria would be with them—but what was she like? Dark, light, tall, thin?

The train began to pull away, to pick up speed, but he didn't see the old woman when the windows began to slide more and more quickly past him, so he smiled at all of them, waved goodbye to everyone, figuring that she'd see him.

Once the gate was behind him, he smiled and thanked the porter once more. Earlier, in July, on these very streets, the nocturnal riot of Carnival had reigned. He joined the loud throng. Bus horns goaded along a float that was trying to make the Avenida del Puerto. There were two white towers with little circular balconies on which panting, half-naked girls danced. On the platform of the float, musicians traded instruments around, ran from one side of the float to the other, excited by the crowd's happy cheers. The float passed beside him. He could see up close the sweating bodies of the musicians and the girls' lovely legs. Then, as now, he felt a rasping thirst. He found the familiar door of Tres Hermanos. The bar was almost deserted; four or five customers sat on the available stools.

The bartender served him a double rum. He told Gregorio that there was plenty of ice out in the Carnival and complained (since he was a true child of socialism and didn't act out of any dirty profit motive) that he didn't understand how some people could prefer an isolated bar to mixing with the cheer of the crowd in the streets. He looked at Gregorio for agreement. From time to time he interrupted himself to pour a drink. Gregorio wanted him to go on talking, protesting, complaining, dictating norms that were to his own advantage, even if nobody paid any attention to him—because a bar is a sort of frontier where opposed languages and interests come together. Let this lugubrious border guard protest, so long as he doesn't stop filling up the glasses!

Gregorio aimed directly at his head, never taking his eyes off him; he squeezed the trigger. Around him, bursts of laughter exploded. The bartender opened a bottle of icy soda, but said you had to go out into the Carnival to get ice. Gregorio aimed at him again. He shot and shot again that talkative, stubborn mouth.

Empty or packed, well or ill tended, a bar is always a bar. One can think there, daydream, travel. High up, flanked by two columns of bottles, the mirror glowed like a lake. He sank into it. He felt wet and revived. He drank again, avidly, waiting for the pleasant lucidity of alcohol to begin vibrating in his head like a flame. Liquor was the only thing that could fill his emptiness, give him spirit, inflame him with a rudimentary joy, calm his restlessness. At his third drink he toasted the baby, for the happy coincidence that they both were fed from bottles. Then he thought of Gloria, who would be upset if he was late coming home. He went to the telephone and called. Her tense voice answered. Yes, he had sent the old lady off. On the train they'd planned. Perfectly comfortable. He'd be back right away. He'd try to get a taxi.

When he got back to his stool and drank the rest of the drink and looked for the bartender to order another, he found him involved in a curious display before a group of customers who were attentively watching him. The bartender poured a little soda on a fly which had lit on the bar. The insect seemed dead, drowned, but all of a sudden lightly moved its wings and flew away. Everyone laughed uproariously; some applauded.

The bartender said they could put a fly in a pail of water and cover it with a newspaper and, when they went back to work, uncover the pail and exactly the same thing would happen. Gregorio stared fixedly at the group gathered in the bar. They were animated, sweaty, happy. In his imagination he saw them suddenly calm, wrapped in overcoats, smiling in repose. Outside, it was snowing. Borodino Bridge was covered with snow. He crossed it hurriedly and turned toward Smolenskaya Nabreznaya.

"Listen, who kills the scorpion?" asked the bartender.

The chorus cried, "The lady scorpion." The bartender bet a bottle of Caney for anyone who could give him the right answer.

"A matter of time," one man yelled. "He probably dies of old age."

But the bartender shook his head, while the open-mouthed chorus waited.

Outside, the day was once again splendid. The sun shimmered on the puddles. He clouded it over and scattered hundreds of birches along the depopulated avenue. He filled the avenue with a different people.

"The cockroach, gentlemen!" the bartender exclaimed. "That's who eats up the scorpion. He stands in front of it and tickles its hump, and when the little man goes to scratch it with the stinger, that's it!" Bursts of laughter filled the narrow room. Gregorio tuned the voices. It was like listening to music or listening to rain. Soon, out in the rain, he spotted Gloria's little convertible. She was soaked and he signaled her, lovely in her radiant anger, to go back home. Beside her, waving his hands in the gusts of wind, the baby gurgled and paddled the raindrops.

The bartender was right. All the ice was at the Carnival. Great smoking blocks were stacked up in the kiosks, and the people who worked in them were beginning to show up. People went in and out of the improvised restaurants, especially La Piragua, brimming over with fricasseed lamb, black beans with rice, and those special Cuban tamales. Behind the bars that stretched in every direction were the nickeled beer chests and tall waxed-paper cups. From the Hotel Nacional the scene took on a studiedly choreographed aspect. The Malecón, like a stage, crowned the reefs, and the waters of the bay glowed against the sunset.

The floats began to move off toward El Morro Castle. La Estrella's was decorated with seaweed and other marine plants. High on it, a blond, slender teenage girl dressed in white, smiling but not at ease, waved at the applauding crowd. Gregorio looked all around. Hands vied to seize frothy cups, heads ducked and puffed— trying to get the foam off the beer, drinking with gusto; other people came out of restaurants with plates full of food and looked for a place to sit on the low circular walls of the plazas. Teenagers wandered about in groups, keeping time to the music, moved by one frenzy, sluffing their feet, swaying like little kids.

His eyes panned across the scene; the smoky mass on

the horizon undulated on the reddened water like a jellyfish. He felt happy to be here contemplating the spectacle from the cement wall that circled the hotel playing grounds. He tried watching the scene from various angles. He looked toward the beer and squid kiosks, only a few yards from him. A group of tourists tried to make themselves understood. The vendors smiled and made signs. Finally they got beer, squid, tamales. He saw them merge into the crowd, accompanied by the boys and girls who had spontaneously become their host.

He wanted to prolong, hold the impression of the scene; but an explosion made him turn suddenly. The crowd was circling around two floats. On them, wrapped in silver gauze, girls agilely swayed to the beat of the music. He panned his eyes again. There was a flux and reflux, a sort of chaotic stained-glass window of fanciful, irregular forms. He opened and closed his eyes several times, fascinated, and breathed deeply as though inhaling a drug. Why had he always, from the time he was a boy, beheld these spectacles with terror, bewilderment, never with joy? Why had he never been cheered by them like everybody else? Who was he, really? Were there people condemned to passive enjoyment, to anticipation that could only be satisfied at a distance, in the act of observing, analyzing, seeing? Now bouquets of multicolored lights exploded in the sky that had suddenly become dark, without his noticing.

He got home late. Trying to move so that Gloria wouldn't hear him, he went cautiously toward his mother-in-law's room. He turned on the light and experienced the joy of knowing it was empty. The old woman would be snoring now in her train compartment.

Other people would see to greeting her tomorrow on the platform, taking her to another bedroom, listening to her interminable stories, tolerating her disgusting habits, but this bedroom had no sign of her now. Its only reminder was this strict, unvarying orderliness. He closed the door and went to the kitchen. He opened the refrigerator and drank a glass of water; then he went to the room he worked in and fell into the armchair, worn out. He felt drunk. On the desk—a long, polished, black slab on sawhorse legs—were the typewriter, his collection of Japanese novels, and the immaculate notebooks that Gloria had set out for him that morning. The lamp made the surface of the desk gleam like the face of a mirror, undulant from the effect of the light. Coming toward him from a remote point, growing larger and larger, huge, with light shining through her, he saw Nuria beckoning him to pass through the surface.

"Come."

Set down among trees that surrounded it as though they were a hedge of foliage, the dormitory seemed haloed by an unreal light. Nuria pushed at the wooden door. Gregorio hesitated.

"Come. There's no one here," Nuria insisted.

And when he was inside, standing in the narrow, desolate hallway, he heard a nasal, revolving, almost infinitely repetitive cry that froze him:

Cálamus

Cálamus   *Cálamus*   *Cálamus*

Cálamus
Cálamus
Cálamus

[3 0]

He looked up. Moored to the lower edge of its iron ring, multicolored, teetering like a lantern on a stormy night, a parrot repeated endlessly, in every imaginable tone of voice, making Gregorio's head spin, that one word which drilled at his eardrums:

Cálamus
Cálamus
Cálamus

"What is that?" Gregorio asked, disconcerted. Nuria laughed.

"They're dactyls, Mr. Writer, just dactyls. I've been saving dactyls to welcome you. Freshly minted dactyls like gállopoid, cláppenstick, lóopity. They're for you, Mr. Writer."

She went on laughing like a girl. A cold sweat bathed Gregorio's body, his strength was about to give. The parrot began repeating the dactyls, alternating them in endless delirium.

"Hush, Panchón," Nuria said to him, and the bird fell silent. Gregorio sighed, exhausted by alcohol and that incessant *ritornello*. Compassionately, Nuria led him to the far end of the dormitory, where he could sit down; but she remained standing, svelte and firm. And ungraspable, unembraceable. What could he say about her, about all the girls like her? How could he ever comprehend those beings always beyond his reach, joined in a community of tasks, worries, enthusiasms, and dreams from which he was excluded? No, the poor annotations he had made of a few weeks in a girls' camp were worthless, ridiculously fragmentary, rhetorical, false.

[3 1]

Nuria went on swaying impatiently, in a kind of desperation. "Tomorrow we'll give you an official welcome. At the camp and here," she said, smiling. "You're a worthy man, an estimable man, Gregorio. It isn't easy to make yourself over from the inside out, but you try. And in the end, the only thing that matters is that you see. *See,* do you understand? It sounds simple, but it's a tough job."

She waited for him to say something, but then added, "Are you very tired?"

He nodded.

"Can you do it or not? Will you try or not?" she demanded.

He nodded again.

Nuria looked at him with concern. "Then what are you thinking about? Why do you look so confused?"

"I was thinking about the dactyls," he stammered.

"Oh, you liked them!" she exclaimed, smiling.

"They're really phonemes, though, aren't they?"

"Really phonemes. Inanities that you might build a meaning out of." She sighed. "But they're so pretty! Don't you think they're like birds, the way they just take off, gárrulous túrtledoves, or swállowtails?"

Gregorio looked at her, puzzled. "But why not anapests or iambs, why not trochees? Why do they have to be dactyls?"

"Because they're ours, Gregorio." Her tone became serious. "Because they don't exist in any other language; because they're gregárious impératives. For example: Thínk of it . . . Spéak to me . . . Cóme to me . . ."

"Those are, well, comminatory . . ."

She stopped a moment, waiting for him to go on. He remained silent.

"You see? Simple words are what you fear. Why do you say comminatory instead of imperative? What world would there be without the simple words? Tell that tree to stop growing or bearing fruit. Nonsense. In this world, only what's natural, simple, survives. We girls here are natural. Our intensity is selfless and constant."

She spoke with a serene and moving self-assurance; Gregorio felt like a dinosaur, worn down by all sorts of erosions, an anonymous, dispossessed relic. Even Panchón the parrot seemed to him an incredibly beautiful repetition machine, dominating the summer sky with its luxuriant, essential plumage.

Nuria noted his breakdown, turned toward him with quiet, beatific pity. Gregorio thought he saw, however, an inquisitive look in her eyes, thought he heard imperious words in her mouth —but it only emitted elevated dactyls, túrtledoves about to fly, swállowtails that bounced off his half-closed eyelids, that fluttered carefree in the sad ashes of his bones.

Gloria's worried voice woke him from his nap.

"What are you doing, Gregorio? Why don't you come to bed? Are you writing?"

"I'm coming."

He stood up, turned off the light, and went into the bathroom. He rinsed out his mouth several times, trying to wash away the smell of alcohol; then he undressed and began to go over his clothes, under the raw, intense light the fluorescent bulbs threw over the material. He scrutinized them down to the most imperceptible abrasion on the fabric, the lightest scuff. He wanted to make sure there was no casual mark that might make her jealous. He didn't find any. He washed his face and stood automatically before the enormous bathroom mirror. Once again he discovered the terrific disproportion of his belly; it consoled him that at least his skin was tight and unwrinkled. He couldn't help thinking of old age. What would his old age be like, exactly? At what moment would he lose the intensity of desire? What would life be like without making love? Would the placidity of Puppy's old master come with the years —Puppy, the little toy dog that reached only high enough to sniff at the bitches in heat but couldn't lift himself to their height? Would she go on loving him, and he her, when they couldn't even sniff at each other in desire, or would they both, at the same time, come to the calm that they say holds old lovers together when love settles into memory, into pure memory? Or would there be a morbid anxiety feeding on the very impossibility of love? Ah, answers! Only time gives answers. A person can imagine being happy or miserable, what life would be like in Paris or Cairo, how he might act in a disaster; but youth doesn't bargain for old age, doesn't imagine it, not even at the beginning of middle age. It's like death. He hurriedly put on his pajamas and went into the bedroom. Gloria asked what time it was. He told her and she scolded him because it was so late. He lay down beside her.

"You've been drinking."

"A beer."

"I can imagine. You always find some excuse. When it's not taking Mama to the train station, it's some friend that shows up, but you always come in at the same time, with the same stench of liquor."

"I felt like that character in Sartre—the condemned

of Altona. I hardly knew the streets. And I was bored,"
he lied; but instinctively he experienced the sharp
drowning sensation, the eternal feeling of guilt.

"What are you thinking about?" she asked.

"Nothing."

"Why don't you go to sleep?"

"This terrible heat."

"You're always hot. I'm cold."

In the half light of the bedroom, this ceiling joined
the other one, decorated with Viennese designs. He took
off his coat as he entered. There was no one at home.
He rubbed his hands together over the radiator. He
went to the double-glazed window and looked out
toward Smolenskaya Square. Finally he saw Tatiana
appear, old and solid, with big black boots and the wool
scarf that almost completely covered her face, like a wig.

"Have you ever thought of wearing a wig?"

"A wig?"

"You never thought of it?"

"Since when are you interested in wigs? Did you see
some woman in a wig on the street?"

"I don't know. It isn't easy to recognize them."

"It might be a good thing if you'd get interested in
women with wigs. Did you see anybody you knew?"

"Nobody."

"I just had a terrible nightmare."

"When?"

"Before you got here. A man was chasing me. He
wanted to kill me."

He felt an irrational chill, dread.

"He wanted to kill me," she insisted uneasily.

"When? What time?"

"What difference does it make what time?"

"I don't know. None, I suppose."

"But it worries you."

"Why?"

"You're almost psychic."

"I don't think any man is after you to kill you. It was a nightmare, that's all."

"But it does worry you?"

"It doesn't worry me. Don't talk nonsense."

But it did bother him. Recently she had these nightmares, which barely masked her most secret obsessions and fears. He would schematically and superficially analyze the dream for her and she would laugh perfectly innocently.

He tenderly stroked her hair.

"Nightmares are terrible," she said.

"Yes, they're terrible."

"I'm going to start taking phenobarbital again to avoid nightmares."

"Yes," he repeated.

"I don't mind dreams, but nightmares are terrible."

He kissed her and she fell silent. He thought again of the hubbub of the Carnival, of the streets, of the young people playing and singing with healthy, contagious enthusiasm; but immediately he thought again of old age and imagined it as terrifyingly futile and corrosive, so he decided to think about youth, but he couldn't stop there. He slid through years and countries, planes and airports. Then he decided to think about middle age. He wondered if Gloria thought about it. What was she thinking about?

"Are you still thinking about the nightmare?"

She didn't answer. He pulled his head back from her shoulder. She was asleep. He looked at her a long time.

He watched her as keenly as, minutes before, he had sought spots on his clothes. He wondered if innocence didn't have some of the same cunning that dreams' censorship did, if there didn't exist some hidden link between the two.

She told him in the morning that he was living the unhealthiest life imaginable, always with his nose in a glass, on the very fringes of nature. She seemed pompous. He mentally suppressed "imaginable," "glass," "fringes of nature," and reduced it to a short, effective reproach: "You're living the unhealthiest of lives," which he admitted. He had always dreamed of a healthy life and envied people who lived that way; but the only healthy existence he dreamed of now was many miles away, among the thousands of tall, solid birch trees lining the white plains and prairies outside Moscow. He had glided across them so many times skiing, in the great immobile cold which stirred only when he pirouetted around the tree trunks, that his health had been transformed into nostalgia. A furious sickly will was all he had left of that now, and he could not make it master the present, could no longer make it accept reality.

He was not living a healthy life. It was a discovery he made every morning when he woke up. Not because she reminded him of the sad way he looked last night, but rather because when the effect of the alcohol wore off, he felt the ponderousness of his body, his lack of lucidity, his depression, his irascibility, his dull anguish.

But she reappeared more capable and chatty every morning. She piled up evidence against him; she armed herself with his skinniness, his weakness. She made him reconstruct the previous night inch by inch; he couldn't have done it without her help. She became a kind of furious archaeologist, throwing up to him his own shameful skeleton, his ugly prehistory.

There were many people who expected his smashup, who had bet on her, who were always ready to cheer her on. He was going crazy. He hid the pages he wrote, so she couldn't read them. She didn't care about that; what she cared about was that he write, that he overcome his sickness, that he fight it, that he not go over to its side. Her eyes were full of tears. He, mute, anguished, heard her from the bed. Suddenly he felt a yank on his hair that produced a surprising relief. He turned over and saw his son smiling at him, still pulling his hair. He raised him from the crib and put him on top of him, on his empty, burning stomach. He felt nauseated. He laid the baby down to one side.

He put on his glasses, and Gloria and the boy came neatly into focus before him. Everything assumed its own shape, without the fuzzy blur of myopia.

Once more he had to agree with her. Though he always made the same vow, and then didn't keep it, there was no doubt that this way of life was destroying him.

She went to the night table and picked up the baby's bottle and a cup. She had gotten up quite a while ago. He saw her face, washed and fresh, her combed hair. Then he turned away and saw himself full-length in the lower mirror of the dresser—that greenish-yellow face, those eyes with their swollen lids behind the thick eye-glasses, that head of tousled hair like straw, that horrible whole that had made him cry as a child.

2

He had promised Gloria to fight his sickness. The old woman would go for two or three months to Gloria's brothers and they themselves would take care of the baby and he would impose an iron working schedule on himself; but from the first he was painfully aware that he could no longer react as he wished. For too many years he had practiced this miserable sloth, this indiscipline; the fact that it was uncomfortable made it nonetheless soft, nonetheless idle. He was thinking this now, as he did the exercises that were part of the plan.

"They're good, too, to keep you young," she said.

He didn't want to tell her that these concerns were typical of middle age. There is no conscious freshness. Youth by definition does not know what its own nature is. She was holding his legs down, so the exercises to reduce his belly would be a little easier for him. He had to lift himself up at least ten times from the horizontal where he lay, with his hands joined behind his head, straining to sit up and touch his knees.

"Don't bend them," panted Gloria. "Try not to bend them."

There on the floor was that grotesque, languid

elephant, realizing that the years had recently added up and made an implacable impression on his body. Who the hell could push himself to that tenth and last movement, except some kind of superman!

He stood up, staggering. She shouted that he had to go on, "no excuses, no whining," at least ten pushups, and after that, come on, bend over and touch your toes —right hand to the left, left to the right. Eagerly, she counted the movements.

He stopped, hesitating, between the door to the last bedroom and the archway to the dining room. He pleaded with her that he'd done enough for today.

"In a month you won't have a bit of fat. Mama won't recognize you." She bent over the crib. "Right, baby?" She picked up the baby.

He tumbled onto the bed again. He turned on the air conditioner and the room filled with an atmosphere of relief. He thought again of Moscow, the Izmailovo wood. In his imagination he added cool morning air, a carpet of leaves, birds, her, the baby, to the scene. He watched them in silence from a hiding place behind a birch tree. He took ten years off his age, ten years off hers, but not the baby's. He added one to his. Now he was two. He liked that age. The three of them were dressed in heavy clothes—she in blue, the baby in red. They both wore berets, and he had on his old black shapka. He pointed out to them the places that were in his memory and his homesickness, as it were; he decided to take her everywhere, to the most distant spots. She sat on a bench to rest then, and he held the baby and listened to her breathe, in the spring of one of the landscapes he had most loved in his life. Thus he heard her breathe in all the seasons and the three of them stopped in the one he liked best—the big long beautiful clean Russian winter. She would caress the snow as though she were clutching coins that dissolved between her thumb and forefinger. Her eyes glowed with happiness, and the baby adjusted to the seasons as though he had always known them. He thought of the houses they had lived in, would live in, of the friends they had had, or would have. Very late at night, so the baby couldn't hear them, they made, that is, would make love, with no shadow of grief, simply happy.

"And a page before eleven o'clock at night."

She was changing the baby's diaper.

"Just think that it's only one a day, you know."

He stretched, aching. He carried many too many pounds, gathering grotesquely at his belly, on his face.

"The punishment will be that you write two for every one you don't do."

He didn't think he was capable of going on with his vow. Today he couldn't write half a paragraph. He would try, anyway. She was content to hear him peck at the typewriter for an hour. Later, as a reward, he could read some book or other. *The Queen of Spades*, by Pushkin, was helping him along. Forty-some-odd pages of ingenious story, told simply, somewhere between Balzac and Maupassant. He only needed to do the page.

"See how pretty the leaf is?"

"What?"

"That leaf, see how pretty?"

He saw through the window the just-sprouted leaf, a tender green color, in the strong light. He stared at it fascinated, as though he were seeing a leaf for the first time, but also with an ineffable pity. He asked himself how that little, just-sprouted leaf could withstand the scorching weather.

He would write the page after his bath. If words didn't come to him, he'd seize any old book and take apart and change around paragraphs as he used to do with pieces of music for the music classes his parents made him take; he'd play them backwards. These little bits of irreverence created a sort of fame as a composer for him among his classmates. The notes to Beethoven's "Für Elise," played backwards, sounded a little like Weber, a certain slovenly, juvenile Weber. Still more unusual effects could be achieved with the paragraphs of a book. Once he did it with a poem by Villon. "I die of thirst beside the fountain" became "The thirst of the dead side of the fountain." And he said that was the real exegesis of Villon's poem.

"Beyond a certain point, every attempt at art is nothing but a parody," he said bitterly. "All so-called originality is a kind of palimpsest. Every word, every sentence, every idea is sullied from its constant use by men. The whole little chorus of literati puffing and huffing with their paragraphs, trying to get their ideas all lined up, to find a subject, to create, to believe they can create—just plagiarizing, the wretches. And trying to call things by any other name is just hiding, disguising, blurring the only possible image, which has already been used a thousand times if it's been used once."

He thought all this but didn't say it. It was a shoddy nihilism, one more alibi for shirking. He should write that page about something, not against something—which might as well be his epitaph. From the depth of the past, the only voice that infused him with confidence was his grandfather's. He had been tall and well built, under the arbors he had planted himself, showing him the wild filly which each of his grandsons had to try to tame in the newly plowed field, where the ground was soft enough to risk it.

"Don't say you can't overcome your fear, because if you think you can, then you leave that possibility open to yourself." He remembered being on the animal, pulling the reins to one side to turn the filly so she would tire and finally surrender. His feet gripped the cinch, but in the end he flew several yards, picked himself up happily, covered with dirt and grass as his grandfather held him. Undoubtedly he had known, like the great Latin poet, that the man who conquers is he who can because he thinks he can.

He felt revived by the shower; he dried off and dressed and went straight to the typewriter. He sat before it as before a machine gun.

"What time is it?"

"One-thirty," Gloria answered from the first bedroom.

"Two," said Nuria from the balcony.

"Two?"

"I said one-thirty . . ." Gloria repeated a little louder.

"Two," said Nuria insistently as she passed through the glass door.

"Did you hear me? It's one-thirty," Gloria repeated loudly.

"Two o'clock sharp," said Nuria, so close to him he could feel her breath on his face. "I've come to get you. Come."

He followed.

.   .   .

Part Three

Before he went to the hotel to take the traveling case, Julio tried to get in touch with Luisa. At the Ministry they informed him that she had left two hours earlier and probably would be just now getting back to her house; but he was calling from "her house." He spoke offhandedly to the receptionist, so as not to arouse her curiosity, though she seemed to have a kind of mistrustful insinuation in her voice that he'd never noticed before. Women are expert, he thought, at detecting those masculine fears that arise even in the most stable marriages. No one believed in those marriages, they sensed behind them a fundamental, almost friendly disharmony, an active jarring.

He wondered where the hell Luisa had gone. Then he shrugged and left her a note. He went downstairs, trying to stay out of sight of his curious neighbors. He was tired of the pompous sympathy of those old croakers, always walking through the yards, snooping out whatever was going on, morbidly spying on neighboring houses, which were, almost all, occupied by young students.

He saw old Zaida, standing in front of the big mirror

in the dining room of her house, patiently putting old yellow rollers in the hair she'd just had dyed, while Fernández Junco was cutting back the root of an orange tree. He felt relieved to have been able to get in the car without being seen. He hurriedly started the engine, but when he turned the car to head toward the Quinta Avenida, he discovered Gregorio Suárez gazing down on him from his window overlooking the street. Gregorio was thin, lazy, too potbellied for his years. Most of the time he spent up there smoking, sometimes while he typed, other times while he abstractedly watched the street. They called him "the Russian" because he had spent some time in the Soviet Union. One day he was suddenly installed in one of the many apartment houses in the Miramar section. He lived with his wife, a child a little under a year old, and his mother-in-law. They were cordially distant and unspeaking. The only noise that was ever heard in that house was the typewriter. Fernández Junco swore that the man had been put there to report on the "life and miracles," as he put it, of the few "decent people" who kept on resisting in Miramar.

"He's a swine. He smiles even at me when he comes out of that cave, and that Gloria of his and her mother are a couple of sweet ones, too. And the little kid looks like a real little communist pigeon. Doesn't even cry."

Zaida maintained good relations with the two women of the house so she could shamelessly sift through their lives. She affirmed that Gregorio was an alcoholic; she had found piles of empty rum bottles in the garage of the house and had heard him lurching and stumbling up the stairs sometimes. The students had their version of his story, too—he was being punished for political reasons, but he was a good comrade who was trying hard to reform. He was being helped: "He's a writer."

Fernández Junco jeered. "A writer! What kind of shit can that old bird write? Reports on all of us, that's all! Let me put mine out, my *Doctor García*! Better than Pasternak's! When 'Patilla' sees it, he'll be so pissed he'll swell up like a frog!"

Along the Quinta Avenida the clear warm sun of early December heightened the color of the trees, the hibiscus blossoms, and the poinsettias. The night before, a few winter gusts had blown in and a light surf had begun to wash over Havana's flat jetty wall, but today it was again sparkling and warm.

In the hotel they told him there was no Swedish guest, no Ona. But he himself had brought her from the airport! "I am her official interpreter." Still, Ona's name didn't appear anywhere on the guest list. "You don't remember the room number, or her last name?" The clerk was becoming a little heated. Julio showed him the bag she had left in his car and repeated that he had brought her to the hotel himself, that he had been her interpreter for the first-shift clerk. This clerk told him rudely to wait until the next day then, and Julio shouted that it was all part of the stinking bureaucracy that was strangling the country, slammed his fist down on the desk (while the tourists stared), and pushed his way through the great mahogany-and-glass doors that closed in the lobby like a stifling aquarium. Russians, Bulgarians, Czechs congregated there, sweating freely even in the central air conditioning—heavy, panting men and women, simple technicians dumped on the beaches of Cuba in compliance with the formal ex-

changes of internationalism. It never occurred to anyone
to ask whether they did their jobs well; what mattered
was that Cuba's existence should be recognized on the
continents, in the world (the eternal insecurity of
islands), that there should be links, that planes should
take off and land in Cuba. Therefore, the hotels endlessly hummed with political conjecture. Since 1959,
hotels crammed with tourists had been Cuba's public
forum.

Outside, the contradictory weather of the island was
still debating with itself whether a cool sunrise might
become an asphyxiating afternoon. Now one of those
downpours was occurring that no weatherman ever fore-
sees, unless it is hurricane season. The car was parked
just a few yards away, but to run even that short distance, those few seconds, in a cloudburst like this would
soak him through.

He was about to sprint off anyway when a voice
stopped him. "You're going to get soaked." It was a man
who had been watching him during his altercation with
the clerk.

Physically he didn't fit the usual image of a Cuban—
he was tall and had straight blond hair, blue eyes, chin
a little too prominent. He was dressed in a style peculiar
to the foreigners. Julio saw immediately that he was a
State Security agent. They filled the hotels, mixed in
with the tourists, pretending to be just another visitor
to the island, but their keen, alert expression betrayed
them. At least, it did to Julio.

The country's old racial prejudice, which the Revolution hadn't eliminated, identified the police with blacks
or mulattoes, never with the physiognomy of a member
of the old aristocratic sporting clubs. But in the new

agents they were recruiting types ideal for operating among probable enemies, people of their own class, unlikely to arouse suspicions. During the years that Julio had put into performing duties of considerable responsibility for the government, news would come to him of the surprising actions of old school friends, once apolitical and insensitive to any feeling of social justice, now acting as Cuban agents abroad, infiltrating counter-revolutionary organizations and U.S. intelligence organs. By doing that, they expunged their class origins, their compromising bourgeois connections—and they revenged the resentments of their student days in U.S. universities, where their classmates, more or less WASPs, designated them by that genteel pejorative "Latins." Now these "Latins" were expert in the idiosyncrasies and weaknesses of the social mechanisms of their ex-classmates.

"I was there when you brought the girl in. The clerk is a bureaucrat. You said it—the bureaucracy is going to strangle us all."

Right down to the accent, he might be an advertisement for a private university. The man tried to be friendly, but in that false cordiality with which he repeated Julio's exact words Julio could hear the quotation marks of a report, the grotesque satisfaction of the *agents provocateurs*. Julio ran to the car without replying.

As he drove toward the Malecón, he thought about the man. He stopped at the light at Calle Línea. On one side he saw one of the billboards that this year were celebrating the anniversary of the triumph of the Revolution. They had put them up everywhere. Zaida and Fernández Junco had remarked on them two days ago. One had been placed on the most visible corner of the

Quinta Avenida, a few yards from his own house. Under the slogan "They point the way" was painted the face of Eduardo, dead a year before the coup, in one of those confrontations between students and police. It was a tactic they were using for the first time—amalgamating the first martyrs in the struggle with Batista with the ideological polemics of the present, lumping everything into one action, a single ideology.

Eduardo looked strong and full of life, with the same intense power in his eyes and in the languid smile that he had in the photo Luisa had kept in the apartment she had lived alone in. Where had she put it? At the beginning of their affair, the photo presided over the living room like a dead brother's, and Julio had never really paid any attention until January 1, 1959, almost at midnight of the single most memorable day of his life.

The night of December 31, 1958, Humberto got him out of bed. The whole cell he belonged to was present; the most distant leaders had friendly faces; they embraced each other, young and old, boys and girls, almost children. And when he left the meeting in which each one had been assigned his particular task, he hadn't wanted to go back home, so he had walked the streets awhile, feeling part of the joy of the crowd. From the sidewalk along the Malecón, he heard the hum of the whole city, he let himself be carried along by the human tide, he walked to Maceo Park and went on to the Avenida del Puerto. The boats of Casablanca were decorated with the red-and-black flags of the 26th of July movement, and on the bay they were singing songs of the Revolution that before that night had been heard only in secret. This, finally, was freedom!

When he came to the plaza of the Cathedral, where

the Paris Restaurant was, excited choruses broke out; as he was halfway across the plaza, he heard someone call his name. In front of one of the doors of the Cathedral, a girl was waving excitedly at him. Luisa. Again. Her beautiful, young, delighted face. They embraced like old friends.

She invited him to her studio, above the restaurant. A pretty place, comfortably decorated, with colonial features—shutters and stained glass. She had created there a kind of sketch of her theory of Cuban architecture, organic to the country, which she had more than once expounded to him. I do like it, he told her; the intelligent, sensible atmosphere of the studio pleased him. Then he saw the photo of Eduardo for the first time and noticed the suddenly sad face of Luisa.

"He never got to know this happiness, Julio. And he was the tenderest, noblest man in the world." He listened to her without taking his eyes off the photograph.

"A drink?"

"Yes, let's have a drink."

She got two whiskies and sat next to him in the armchair.

"To freedom," they said, almost at the same time.

She looked at the picture. "We were going to have a baby."

It was the last time they talked about Eduardo; afterwards they talked about her plans. She wanted to tell him her ideas for the construction of workers' housing in the Cuban style which the architect Porro had introduced. She loved the tall buttresses, lots of vegetation all around, stained-glass windows that attenuate, sift the light as the colonial Spanish architects had used them, to serve the reality of the country, not aping Spanish peninsular styles. Months later, when the affair had become intimate, as it was inevitable that it would, the picture disappeared.

It had been Julio, curiously, who had been given the responsibility by the Revolutionary movement of telling Luisa of the death of Eduardo. He had done it strictly as a duty, for he had had no personal association with Eduardo, nor had he known him at the university, as he had so many others. Humberto and Cuca had cried with rage and impotence when they saw him bleeding in the car that Julio tried to drive as fast and carefully as he could to the private clinic the organization used in these situations.

Ten years gone by, and yet the serene, languid face of Eduardo, exactly reproduced next to the year's motto, had not been touched by time. Nothing had marred that twenty-year-old's face; Julio would never see twenty again.

Luisa said nothing when she saw the billboard. She looked at Eduardo's image as though it were the face of any other martyr. She behaved like a man for whom the memory of a woman is just barely part of the past, however intense the link had been. Time finally dissolves women into a dull reality, into vague, diffuse stimuli like those called up by masturbation, the bodies of someone and no one—impersonal, anonymous sex. As time, years go by, however, the image becomes more obsessive, the memory of certain sexual moments reappears over and over, and it stays in the mind through every relationship, every surrender.

Luisa had known, needed, loved the man whom the whole country now cheered and respected. It was the ten years since his death that she no doubt missed. Now they were both entering middle age. She was frustrated, vulnerable, though she struggled to hide it. She would say she was tired, that the long hours in the Ministry of Construction trying to make plans for children's parks tired her. She wanted to present her plans to the Party administration as the economically optimum and educationally superior alternative to Children's Circles, which were simply a continuation of the old methods of the Republic, great repressive hulks. Her project would take advantage of Cuba's climate, the pleasant inclemencies of winds and showers in the tropics. But in recent months he saw in Luisa's fatigue deeper roots. While his sexual desire stayed alive, hers was in a decline; the body he would possess—not as often as he wished—hardly responded to his ardor. How would she have responded to Eduardo?

He looked again, with anguish, at the poster designed by the Office of Revolutionary Orientation, that ministry of information which used only initials, which dared not reveal its name, so people wouldn't remember it had been created by Batista. Eduardo's face, illustrating hundreds of billboards across the entire country, occupied the most visible sites in Havana. A subtle stroke of publicity, like all ORO propaganda—skillful, well executed, as effective as that of the old capitalist public-relations agencies.

As he approached the house, he dreaded that he would find Zaida outside, arranging those old termite- and rust-riddled sticks of furniture that she pulled out when there was nothing else to do. Probably Fernández

Junco would have let the dog out, too, so he could enjoy watching it run crazily around the garden. But when he arrived he didn't see either of them; he could skip having to say hello to them. The anxiety didn't go away altogether. The translations that punctually each week he had to turn in distressed him even more, and now they had dumped on him the responsibility of being interpreter for a Swedish woman who—the last straw— only had German in common with Julio. He accepted the duty that Humberto and Braulio asked him to perform. Nobody in ORO spoke German. What name had Security hidden this insignificant girl under? Maybe he was wrong; maybe she herself had decided to become anonymous. For a long while now, everybody had had a persecution complex.

He got out of the car to open the gate and left the headlights on while he unbolted it. He noticed a cable crackling sparks in the rain, the very one that carried current to the billboard with Eduardo's image. Then he crouched down, looking carefully all around to be sure no one was watching him; he grabbed a rock and threw it at the lights; it shattered them.

He looked around again and smiled in satisfaction. Putting out the lights made the dusk even deeper. The house was dark. Luisa would no doubt be at Braulio and Cuca's house, and he was glad; he would have a few minutes without needing to talk and he would forget the stupid argument at the hotel. But as he started up the walk he was surprised that on the wall next to the garden, the wall that had no bookshelf or even a picture on it on the inside, there was a crack running from one side to the other. Afternoon light poured through it into the house.

❧ 2 ❧

IT WASN'T A MATTER now of sparing her one more moment of distress by emptying the ashtrays, putting things in a modicum of order (above all, washing and putting the coffee cups in their precise place), so she wouldn't have to go through the meticulous fuss that lately drove her to a kind of somber dullness. That flagrant crack, completely unexpected, that was there before his eyes now was too much, not only for her (who, after all, had learned to live with her own anxieties, surrounded by an unalterable schedule of pills), but for him, too. He saw himself suddenly menaced by a new threat of disaster.

Mentally he went over the friends who might respond to his calls. He opened the drawers of the desk and looked for old address books. He found one, filled with names and phone numbers of foreigners, the notebook he least needed right now. He thought of Braulio, of Raimundo, of Humberto. They weren't the best ones to solve the problem, but they might have some idea how to go about it.

Braulio wasn't in. He tried to get in touch with Raimundo but was told he was still in Matanzas.

Humberto's voice from the other side of the city calmed him. He didn't know anyone, but it was possible to find a way to get this taken care of, though December complicated things. Almost no one was in Havana.

"I suppose you can wait a few days."

"I'm terrified of these rains," he said. "I'm afraid the house will cave in on top of us."

"It's a big crack?"

"Really, I hadn't noticed it until now. But it's enormous."

"But you hadn't noticed it before?"

"I saw it when I came in."

"Are they doing any construction nearby?"

"I thought of that myself—no. It's the wall right by the garden. It's a long way from here to the front gate. There's nothing but trees and the house next door, you know, where Fernández Junco and Zaida live. The rest of the houses have students in them."

"Anyway, it can't be that serious, Julio."

"I think it is."

"You're not exaggerating a little?"

"The worst part of it is that it keeps getting bigger every minute."

"The house isn't so old."

"No, but the walls have started to crack and there's at least a quarter of an inch opening."

He could see the day and the trees and the jumbled line of rusty furniture, the swing and the water pump and the Bengal fig, dry and black; but he didn't tell Humberto.

"What really worries me is Luisa."

"You couldn't close up the room for a few days, or at least keep her from going in?"

"That's what I intend to do. But, Humberto, this was all I needed. We've already closed up seven. We practically live in the bedroom and the library. Well, let me know if you can do something."

He hung up and suddenly thought of a temporary solution. Raúl Martínez's painting, a sort of mural sequence, hung on the adjoining wall and was about the same length as the crack. He could cover it up, at least for the first few hours, especially if it didn't rain.

The painting fit perfectly; only from time to time a barely perceptible tremor shook it. "If there isn't too much wind tonight, she won't notice a thing."

Nonetheless, the thought that the change might upset her made his plan less than perfectly satisfying. In the last few months her anxiety had taken very subtle turns. Books, vases, ashtrays always occupied the same place. There was a kind of morbid smugness in that urgent tone that scolded him from above his typewriter.

"Julio."

When he turned, he would see her, irritable, pointing out his error, his slovenliness. It was true. He *always* forgot to spread out his towel after his bath. These minutiae shaped themselves into a kind of ferocious code that finally had come to rule even her most intimate relations. Even in the way he took her (late at night, after tiring hours of translation), she demanded of him a symmetrical, unvarying gasping whose least alteration sent her to the verge of tears.

That picture in a spot not chosen by her could aggravate things. But between closing the library for a few days (which would arouse her suspicions too) and suggesting a change in the position of the picture—on which point he could apply all his strength of persuasion

—he didn't hesitate a moment in opting for the second.

The first thing to do was to turn off the overhead light and turn on the night-light; the second, wait for her in the living room and lead her to the bedroom with the excuse of having the kind of domestic encounter they could hardly have in the library, where students across the way could easily watch them. And then, to keep her in the bedroom under any pretext that came to mind. Turn on the radio to listen to a shortwave broadcast by an old friend in exile. The next day everything would be much simpler. He would walk with her to the bus stop and use the rest of the day to try in every way possible to cover up the crack that was now letting in the splendor of the afternoon sun, making the colors of the oil paint more intense.

Later he thought of a last alternative—creating simultaneous pockets of disorder in various places in the house. He went to the kitchen, drank some coffee, and didn't wash the cup. He stubbed out two or three cigarette butts in the ashtray. He changed the vases around, put books, dictionaries out of place.

He stood awhile contemplating it all and dropped onto the chaise longue with the uncorrected manuscript pages of the terrible translation of Marcuse's *The End of Utopia*—a discussion held at the Free University in Berlin and compiled into a book with every mark of a swindle, for the German-American philosopher had only a few paragraphs at the beginning and some fairly brief responses at the end. The rest was commentary by professors and students.

In spite of the repugnance he felt toward these discussions, which nonetheless he saw himself obliged to translate as faithfully as possible, exactly as they themselves deserved, *this* had been in the last few months his only means of existence. The tedious sessions of German that his mother had imposed on him with such severity (the old Austrian tutor looking at him day after day with professional contempt) were now helping him to avoid starvation on an island alien to his upbringing, an island which, from the time he was a boy, had only touched some of his senses—smell and hearing: stinks and body odor, banging and racket. The rest was a kind of brazen sculpture—jaundiced gesturing men, and big words.

He felt hardened and cynical, for these frequent thoughts ended up humiliating him. This warm savage island was his—his hostility and contempt were no better, really, than the failings he was always deploring. His own unlove spawned those evils.

Did the German philosopher know this who spoke of the Third World with words whose nuances called to mind old adorations of the noble savage, the cult of the primitive life, nostalgia for the young peoples of the world?

Julio had promised Humberto to do the translations and turn them in without comment. ("You can't afford any sort of confrontation," he had said.) Raimundo would enthusiastically read the just-translated paragraphs and look at him as though inviting him to share his enthusiasm. He would hardly react, displaying an indifference that might be mistaken for modesty, in his effort to hide his disdain.

One day he gave his opinion and Raimundo was vexed, perplexed by it. He began to pace his office like a character in a play. "I can't see why you're objecting. What do you think is wrong with it?"

When he told him, they became entangled in a discussion that lasted for hours. When he returned home, his mouth was dry, his temples throbbed, his eyes were fevered. He turned on the desk lamp and took up Marcuse's book again. Every paragraph inspired new disproofs. He was irritated with himself for leaving out even more solid arguments in the debate, for having made concessions for the sake of conversation.

Now he went over the translated paragraphs again, furiously marking with a red pencil, suggesting lines of inquiry that Marcuse had only skimmed the surface of. "What are his concrete alternatives?" he said aloud. "This pessimist is out to humble a theoretical movement, but he hasn't even managed the least outrageous statements that Korsch has made. Why doesn't he have the nerve to say there's been a Thermidor and 'worker' isn't written with a capital 'W' anymore, or 'State' with a small 's'?"

Sounds at the door drew him from his soliloquy. He jumped up to catch Luisa on the stairs, but it was too late. She came in tired, but with no outward signs of anxiety. Her lynx-like gaze instantly seized on the disorder. He put his arms out to her, stretched her out on the chaise, and lay down beside her.

"It is a mess," she said in her formal-colloquial English. "Have you had visitors?"

"No."

"I don't understand why everything is in the wrong place. It looks as if it's on purpose, to upset me." Her eyes were moist. "I'm not surprised. I called my brother today at the clinic and I'm sure he told his secretary to tell me he wasn't there. 'She's nutty again.' I think you're feeling the same way. I wear you down."

"You always think the worst."

"He was there. The operator put the call through. Everything changed when I told the secretary my name. 'Tell her I'm not here.' The girl was very uneasy. She was lying."

"Why didn't you ask for Nuria?"

"I did."

"Then they weren't there. They had gone to the Circle to pick up the kid."

"At three o'clock in the afternoon?"

"Why did you call him?"

"That lump under my arm is driving me crazy. I didn't want to go to the doctor."

"I told you it's a ganglion infection. I have the same thing."

"I know. I went to the clinic. The doctor didn't want to see me. She said I had to wait my turn; I don't have anything serious. She was angry, rude. Everybody in this country acts as if they're dealing with an enemy. I pleaded with her at least to look at it. She finally did, but she told me she wouldn't give me a prescription."

He pulled her toward him and kissed her.

"Not now, please . . ."

He kissed her again, turning her back to the picture. She was wearing a light dress, easy to take off.

"Not now, please. I haven't had a bath."

He began to caress her and didn't stop until she opened her lips of her own accord, closing her eyes. It was that mute, gasping game—the beginning happy and spontaneous, and the long difficult orgasm.

"You're soaking wet," she said.

"It's the heat."

"No, it's that I take so long."

"Yes," he said with deliberate cruelty, and she turned away, sighing, her head bowed, her hair black, tangled, long.

"I don't understand why you've made these changes," she said softly.

"It bothers me to translate with that bunch of deformed faces in front of me."

"But the vases . . ."

"I went to get some dictionaries. I'm going to put them back."

"They're better there, anyway."

"No, I'll put them back."

"Leave them. Nobody came, really?"

"Well, the landlady. She brought a letter."

"From abroad?"

"Yes."

"That terrifies me."

"Why?"

"Sooner or later, they'll ask about us."

"Tell them you'll do exactly what you please, darling, that you'll live with whomever you please, sleep with whomever you please. They didn't ask your opinion when they left you alone. Tell them the truth."

She stood up. She took the dress and began smoothing it. "Maybe it would be the best thing," she said, and stopped a few steps from the picture. Julio watched her intently. She was still naked.

"Turn around."

"What do you see? Is something on me?" she cried suddenly, twitching.

"A little black spot," he said sullenly.

"Where?"

"I don't know exactly. Turn around."

She began to walk toward the mirror, turning and twisting like a spastic.

"Where?" she cried.

"Here," he said. "Come here."

And he grabbed her by the arm and pulled her toward him, down again onto the chaise.

"Where?"

"Here!" he shouted. "On your stomach, on your breasts, on your thighs, on your back, on your hips. You're covered with black spots!"

She began to laugh. She laughed stridently and openly for the first time, like a girl.

"Your whole heart is black," she said. "You're making fun of me."

He kissed her, squeezing her as though he had pulled her from danger, happy and frightened at the same time. But she managed to sit up, in the same motion covering herself with the dress. "You're not going to start again. Do you want to kill me?"

He stared at her in silence with a dark, languid look.

"You do it like a madman."

"Not yet, but I guarantee you . . ." he said slowly.

"Get dressed, it's late."

"I don't plan to go out."

"We're going to get something to eat."

"I'm not hungry."

"Then to hell with your order. This vase here and this one here." And she began to put the library back into shape. "And these books here and these dictionaries here and these butts over here . . ."

He watched her go into the bathroom and empty the

[6 5]

ashtrays into the toilet and flush it. She came back a while later bathed, fresh, pulling the tangles out of her hair with a brush.

"Go take a bath. I put out your clothes."

Boiling-hot water came out when he turned the taps, and he skipped around like a hare until he had adjusted the temperature. When he came back to the library, she was lying on the chaise, smoking, abstracted, with the ceramic ashtray beside her.

"What are you doing?"

"Nothing."

"Shall we go?"

When they were at the door, she said, "You know something?"

"What?"

"From now on, I'm going to be more flexible."

He looked at her in surprise. "More flexible?"

"To each his own, right? I was trying out ways of hanging the picture."

Julio suddenly turned toward the painting.

"No," she said. "I left it where it was. I moved it several times and I think you're right, because that wall is filthy."

"Filthy?" he repeated slowly.

"Don't try to pretend. That's why you did it. To cover the dirt. Why didn't you just tell me?"

Then he looked at her with—for the first time ever— a strange horror.

✠ 3 ✠

AT THE HEADQUARTERS of the Defense Committee, a big boisterous mob had gathered.

"There must be some kind of meeting this afternoon," Luisa said.

A car stopped in front of the main entrance. The chairman of the committee appeared, leading a pale, thin old woman who was desperately waving her arms. The chairman only said, "Let's go, please," and they got into the car, which raised a cloud of dust as it drove off. At the door, the curious lingered.

"What's happening?" asked Julio.

"You don't know?" someone said. "She was selling her piss."

"They ought to throw some people in the labor camps even if they *are* ready to kick the bucket. Can you imagine selling your piss?" said another.

They explained that it was an old, lucrative business. The old woman was a diabetic and got an extra ration of food—more milk and meat. To receive the extra quota, she had to send in a urinalysis showing she really was sick along with the application. So she got the idea of selling her illness to her neighbors, and the little flasks began accompanying dozens of applications from the same area of the city—a rash, as it were, of diabetics in one area. The committee had found them out.

In the restaurant, Julio still dwelt on the scene. He was pale and could hardly eat. It wasn't the first time he had heard of these cunning little games, these near-perfect acts of defiance with which people quietly subverted rationing.

Luisa squeezed his hand. "Eat," she said, looking into his eyes.

But Luisa's face before him sharpened his desolation. Either the lamp didn't throw off enough light in the room, or in the effort of moving the picture from one wall to the other (which really was too much for her), Luisa hadn't noticed the crack—or she had lied about moving it in the first place, and had simply left the picture where he had put it, with the tolerant generosity women often show toward men's whims. Or perhaps she was sinking deeper and deeper into that detachment, that strangeness that in the last few months had been the most alarming sign of her condition.

He watched her as she abstractedly pulled the bones from the fish. Her hair covered her back but left her broad forehead exposed. Her almost childlike hands, with the short brittle fingernails that embarrassed her, moved dexterously.

He liked to watch her, like that, when she wasn't aware of it—naked or resting, or squatting like a boy in the center of the room, making fanciful combinations, mixing revolutionary propaganda bills and little figures cut out of foreign magazines. She had put one up in the bathroom. "Everybody to the Plaza de la Revolución!"

and immediately a line of touristy exclamation, in English. "In Holland, where the good life begins," with a Dutch girl in full color, her lap full of incredibly vivid flowers. There was another one, patiently assembled, of a stewardess sitting on Uncle Sam's hat, the hat on an enigmatic Goldwater's head, his chest blazoned with numbers and a brief text: I SAW SOVIET CUBA; then a basket of apples and a picture of Mayakovsky, upside down.

He would stare at her fixedly, like one possessed. He would pretend to hunt through the dictionary, he would scribble over the sheet of paper to make her think he was correcting a text, so he could watch her abandoning herself completely to seeking unforeseen effects in the combinations of letters and images. From time to time she would suddenly stop, analyze the grouping, give in to tedium, and let herself fall into the chaise longue a few feet from him, gazing at the ceiling with impatience or with alarm.

He couldn't watch her long without feeling the restlessness born of anxiety which was mixed in him with the most basic jealousy. The more absorbed he saw she was, the more stubbornly he tried to imagine her in her previous life, especially with Eduardo. She hadn't known many men; perhaps fewer than most women knew—but the three or four that had made her theirs were the obsessive focus of his thoughts. He hated the passion she had put into those experiences, the morbid curiosity that had dragged her to those strangers who had only retained from her the surprise of a body inexplicably clumsy for a girl who would go to bed with them direct, no beating around the bush. Then he hated her; he would push away the typewriter to attract her attention, he would answer a question in cutting monosyllables, would go to the kitchen and pour himself a cup of coffee and slam down the cup with an irritation that left her unmoored, out of orbit, floating like an idiot. Her silence, the fear he divined in her silence, only increased his spite. He imagined her elemental, a vixen, frustrated, returned from her adventures clutching at him like a drowning woman.

No matter how mature, how intelligent he was, he would never be able, calmly, to contemplate the inevitable sexual experience of a woman. His understanding had been circumscribed by the way he had been brought up. His eyes closed, feigning fatigue or sleep as he lay sprawled in the big armchair, he would hear her steal away like a cat. She would flee to the bedroom, thinking that her presence during his working hours upset him, and she would half close the door, quietly take off her clothes, and throw herself on the bed, her breathing uneven. He would spy on each of her movements through the narrow slit left by the hinges. This mute battle produced in him a perverse satisfaction, and that, in turn, triggered his defense mechanisms, before which she was crippled, rendered helpless, neuter. He wanted her to know that it was he who set the traps, maintained the distances, he who was forever fleeing, ungraspable, a trickle of water between her fingers, the absolute master of this union constantly threatened, endangered from the outset. He was always finding ways of suggesting this to her, at the beginning in a simple intellectual diatribe, dispassionate and cold: "Marriage is a business contract and the major shareholder is the male." Then he rattled off a list of the frustrated couples they knew, and came at the end to their two names. He maintained that the only union was a sexual one. "And a dry, sad one, at that," he added. "In a few years we'll hate each other."

"Why?" she asked, groaning.

"The ideal thing is to go to bed together, until you manage to bring me off, and then to hell with you."

"I couldn't go to bed with anyone else."

He seized on that sentence and spoke with a deliberate, patient cynicism. "You'll go to bed and you'll do incredible things, just as you do with me. You'll like prostituting yourself, going brazenly from one male to another. Life is like that."

"It's a lie," she said dully.

"They'll screw you like you ask me to screw you. You'll enjoy looking at yourself sideways in the mirror."

"You're a pervert. You're sick."

He became calmer and calmer, took the calm he showed her to an extreme; he became even more sarcastic. "You're afraid of words. Not me. You'll go to bed. I'll go to bed."

"You like making love grotesque, don't you? Making me bitter and making yourself bitter. If you don't love me, tell me."

"Haven't you gone to bed with men before? Other times?"

"I was free. You have no right to judge me from my own confessions. I should never have talked openly to you. I thought you were an adult."

"But I'm a cruel, disgusting romantic, aren't I?"

"I'm so shy, and you make me out to be some rag."

"Shy?"

"Yes, shy."

"You undress, walk around stark naked with the lights on. You want me to do the same thing. And you say you're shy."

"In spite of that, yes, I say I'm shy."

"A whore," he said softly. "That's what you should say. You're a twenty-four-year-old whore, stupid for your age. Too boring and clumsy for your years. Wouldn't it be better to say a little black whore with little round tits?" He began to laugh, pushing her out of bed. "Get out of here, you little moron!" he shouted, and turned his back.

He heard her gasp, cornered. Now she's completely asexual, he thought. He watched her get up, go toward the bathroom and wash her face, naked, sobbing.

He always emerged from these too frequent scenes with a sad calmness. He was tied to this girl by the convulsions and tendernesses that were the only form his love took. She had entered his life when he was too adult, at the very end of his youth, but his thirty-five years brought him no gift of calmness or aplomb; they only brought irritability and alienation. All the prejudices of the adolescent—the cult of the marriage rite, of chastity—were concentrated at his age, had betrayed his lucidity, filled him with angry scruples. He found peace only when he humiliated her, ran her down.

It pleased him to hear her accept his judgments and submit patiently to his diatribes. He took pleasure in playing with the wound, proposing abject situations that she dodged with terror. He would tell her that marriage was disgusting, that to achieve it, the only sensible thing was to buy a virgin and submit her to a sole painful night. And leave her afterwards, if she began to feel pleasure.

Sometimes, when she was silent too long, Julio would stop; he could hear himself preaching like a madman, wheeling around the same obsessions, ashamed and depressed at the same time.

"You've hardly eaten," said Luisa.

"I'm not hungry. Let's go."

They left and got into the car. There was a hot foul vapor inside. Julio started the engine. "My trusty old Opel," he said aloud as he drove toward the Malecón, "you just won't break down. Capitalists made you so we can get socialism moving."

Half of Miramar was dark. Housefronts and dark yards could be glimpsed only fleetingly, lighted by car headlights. When he got to Calle 30 and the Quinta Avenida, everything suddenly lit up, but the park at Calle 24 remained in shadows. The students' houses were lighted by candles. Through the windows could be seen cots and half-dressed girls lying on their beds. A group stuck their heads out when they heard the car pull into the garage. You could hear laughter and whispering.

"Don't they ever get tired of watching us come and go?" said Julio.

"They're just girls, they're bored."

"Well, we must bore them by now. They've been doing this for three years."

He went to the gate and locked it. As they were walking along the wall of the library that gave onto the garden, a shaft of light across the thick foliage of the vine stopped him.

"What is it?"

"Nothing," he said, visibly nervous.

"No, you must see something." She began to move forward.

He grabbed her arm. "I told you nothing."

But she pulled out of his grip and walked toward the fence. "Of course. That light."

"It's nothing."

"What do you mean, nothing?"

"A crack—not important. We can fix it tomorrow, easy."

She went on looking, not listening to him. "It's the library, isn't it?"

"The wall onto the garden, but it'll be easy to fix tomorrow." He spoke with growing distress.

She looked at him strangely. "What are you talking about?"

The question echoed against the wall, louder no doubt because of where they were standing. Now her obsessiveness would come out again. She would burst into tears, her head on his chest, sobbing out of control; he would smooth her hair, caress her forehead and her cheek, part nurse, part psychiatrist, part lover, a kind of multiple angel of mercy.

"Either you left the library light on or somebody else did," she said.

He tried to dissemble. "Maybe your brother. He hasn't given you back the key."

"He wouldn't have stayed five minutes if he saw we weren't here."

He looked at the light again and assured himself that it came from the window. "It's strange that it doesn't show through the crack." But he was glad of it. "Let's go," he said. "I'll bet my life it's your brother."

When they got to the top of the stairs, he rang the bell. They heard music from the other side of the door. It was a Mulligan record. He rang again and heard the volume go down.

"Yes, it must be my brother."

When they opened the door, they saw Humberto lying on the chaise, smoking one of his cigars, with a glass of rum, reading the album cover. Julio recognized the pile of books beside him that he had lent him months ago and had not expected to get back. He also saw that Raúl's painting was a little crooked and that books were out of place.

"What are you doing here?"

Humberto put down the album cover and came toward Luisa. "How are you, Luisa?" He kissed her.

"A little tired, but fine."

He turned to Julio. "Didn't you call me?"

"Yes, but how did you get in?"

Luisa said she was tired; they would end up, just like always, talking about politics, so she was going to lie down for a while.

"I promise tonight at least we won't even mention half a word about the Revolution," said Humberto.

"I hope so," said Luisa as she left, "or you'll both end up in the loony bin."

When they were alone, Humberto lay down again on the chaise.

"She's fine. She doesn't look nervous at all to me," he said. "Whereas you . . ."

"Don't get started," interrupted Julio.

"Really. You look more nervous to me."

"Well, there are a million reasons for me to be."

"I'm not arguing with you, but you do."

[7 5]

"And you've decided to give me a therapy session, right?"

"I came because you sounded desperate on the phone."

"I called you, that's all."

"And I'm here."

"Okay. I appreciate it."

"You don't act as if you appreciate it," Humberto said sarcastically.

Julio began to pace the room, adjusted the painting, and sat down in front of Humberto.

"How did you get in?"

Humberto stood up. "How do you think? Through the crack over there. Through your crack." He looked at him angrily. "You could have saved the bait. If you wanted me to bring your books back, you didn't have to resort to that kind of trick. There they are. Take 'em."

"That's not why I called."

"Then you wanted to play a little joke."

"No, not that either."

"But there's no crack in the wall, Julio. I've looked. I didn't see anything. And if there's no crack but you saw one and called to tell me about it, that means you're going crazy."

"That's possible," Julio said dully.

Humberto started to laugh. "You're crazy. Don't make me laugh."

"I saw the crack and called you."

Humberto went on laughing.

"You don't believe me. But it's absolutely true. I didn't look very carefully, whatever you want, but it's true. There was a huge hole. It seemed to me I could see the garden through it. Maybe I was tired. I had translated for over eight hours. I hadn't eaten all day when I called you."

"You should have eaten something."

"There wasn't anything to eat. Not even eggs."

"Now you're starting to sound like one of those refugee worms. Don't start your worming with me."

"Not even bread."

"And that makes you see visions."

"No, but I'm all fucked up," said Julio softly.

"And it's going to get worse," cried Humberto, "much worse. Listen, Julio, this country has changed. Face it. For better or worse. Face it, you know it. There's no choice."

"Not even for a critical intelligence."

"Not even."

"Then this is bullshit."

"So?"

"Just bullshit!" shouted Julio. "If this situation has no room for a critical attitude, it's just the holiest bullshit. Yes or no?"

"No," answered Humberto serenely. "In spite of everything, it's not. Because this country is plagued with critical intelligences whose only virtue is being a critical intelligence. And that, my friend, is the holiest bullshit."

"But this man is nothing but a revivalist who changes his plans and ideas every time he pisses. This is a country run by this guy's bladder. He reminds me of Henri Christophe. He won't stop until he's made this country into another Haiti. He's obsessed by history. The island isn't enough for him."

"There's absolutely nothing wrong with that," said Humberto. "Since Bolívar, he's the only political genius of the Americas. A hero. Face it."

"It's a sad country that needs heroes," cried Julio.

"Sad or not, there are countries that need them, in spite of what Brecht says."

"Not Cuba."

"Oh, yes, Cuba. The worst of all, the most godless, the most cynical."

"Then it was punishment it needed. That's what has happened."

"That's your opinion."

"Our native Marxists think differently, of course—the neo-Marxists. Created after the Revolution came to power. Ex-Catholics, ex-herbalist necromancers, ex-voodoo priests, all transformed by the heavenly grace of power. And, as far as I'm concerned, as fake and cynical as ever."

Humberto placed his hand on Julio's shoulder. "How are the translations going?"

"Okay."

"But really okay, right?"

"I do everything I can to avoid an argument."

"Are you turning them in on time?"

"Don't worry. Every Friday, I show Inmundicia my face."

"That's what's important. Even if you have to show Raimundo your face, too."

"Just Inmundicia."

"You never liked him."

"He's a jerk."

"Shy. And you attack him, make fun of him, ridicule him constantly. He must hate your guts."

"I give a shit. He's a cretin. He doesn't have an idea in his head, but he moves exactly like an octopus, by thermal reflexes. He's always hanging around with

Americans in the hotel restaurants. He's so attractive to them because he's so helpless—everything always happens to him. The pathological case that Americans love."

"You're talking exactly like the hundred thousand worms in Miami and New York and Puerto Rico," Humberto said. "The poor man does his work, speaks English perfectly, knows the country and can be useful to us in getting things across to the American mentality which are hard for them to understand."

"And which he doesn't understand, either," added Julio.

He seems to be the right man to me. Don't think he spends all his time worshipping them; on the contrary, they're the only ones he loses his shyness with. He becomes a little ironic, talks like a mature man, a lot of times mixing in Spanish words to get across the resentment he feels toward the Third World—he himself says it's underdeveloped. It's moving to hear him say (I got this from the guides at the CIIF,* who told me about it) that he feels like a black from the South."

"If he hasn't eaten one."

"I think he serves a function. And that the Revolution does very well to use him. I'd even go so far as to give him an award, or even make him a member of the Party," said Humberto.

"What this guy and Fernando Cardenal are, are the most cynical people of the century. And you want me to be happy."

"What I want is for you not to damn a whole revolution for tolerating these people."

"I think it produces them."

* Cuban Institute for International Friendship.

"You see?"

"Yes, it produces them."

"These guys lived before, this kind of person does the same thing under any system. For a while longer, they're ineradicable. For the moment, we need the highest degree of loyalty. *That's* what we need."

Then Julio cried that Humberto understood absolutely nothing and that all this rationalizing was the worst sort of cynicism. And Humberto shouted back that a revolution had its implacable laws and that those laws created their own morality, however bitter and unpleasant, and that we should study history, and Julio shouted that history was bullshit—and so they became embroiled in a debate of two deaf men waving their arms. Julio went to the kitchen and poured himself a glass of water and drank it down in a gulp. When he returned, he found Humberto standing watching the flickering of candles in the students' house next door.

He turned around when he heard Julio come back. He was breathing heavily, his eyes were bloodshot, and his stringy black hair covered his forehead like the wing of a crow. When he took a few steps, he seemed to be hopping like a crow.

"You're a fucking crow," Julio said. "You'll wind up eating us all. You guys make yourselves an illusion of science. You think you know the laws of history, and you're nothing but a bunch of fucking crows. How did you get in, my little crow? You still haven't told me."

"We forced the lock. The black students helped me. Didn't you see? They pissed on the stairs. They were all black and they came to pluck out your eyes. They were shouting, 'Where are you, worm, you big wormy grub?'"

[8 0]

Julio was rigid. "Don't joke," he cried. "I won't let you make fun of me."

"All right, here," Humberto said seriously, and handed him a key.

"What's this?"

"You don't recognize the key to your own house?"

"Who gave it to you?"

"Your brother-in-law. He came to see you. He says Luisa telephoned the clinic. There's a letter from her parents. That German came by, too—Günter?"

"Yes."

"I'm going," said Humberto.

A crow. He moves like a crow, he gestures like one, he has all the earmarks of one. Julio watched him open the door, his hand like a wing grasping the brass doorknob; he heard him going downstairs with the furtive hops of a crow, pecking at the steps, leaving a mess of feathers, a great long growing shadow. He's a perfect crow, Julio thought. He crossed the hall between the library and the kitchen. He stopped as he passed the mirror. The mirror gave back his wasted, emaciated, anxious image. "I'm skinny. There's not a doubt I'm getting old. I look like a chinchilla."

In the bedroom, Luisa was lying in the peaceful abandon of sleep, half naked, a book open beside her. He walked toward her, but stopped. He turned off the light and went back to the library. He threw the window wide open. Up from the garden came the sweet pungent smell of the white night-blooming jasmine that grew all over the fence. "I've got to cut the grass, or it'll swallow us."

He lit a cigarette and looked out at the night. In the students' buildings that surrounded his, that made his house a kind of proud, extravagant island, hundreds of boys and girls slept. Within a few hours they would be awake again, running through the rooms in their blue uniforms, their boots thudding, doing exercises, marching military-style to their classrooms, dragging their feet—the girls with their keen voices calling the orders. That would last a half hour. They began at seven, they interrupted his best sleep, when he was exhausted, after he had worked until late, into the early-morning hours. But now they slept, and in the motley rooms there was hardly a sign of life.

The trees fluttering in the night wind threw shadows over the broken panes of the windows, over the cracked and flaking frames of the houses. Everything was falling into ruin.

Almost daily he could see the increasing decay of Miramar—the large solid residences that proclaimed a ten-year abandonment, the gardens full of weeds, the iron benches rusted and rickety, the deserted balconies half destroyed.

But at night the neighborhood recovered its old majesty. Darkness hid the cracks and grime, and from a distance it took on again its old splendor. His own house was sinking too, unsavable. It didn't care about his decision to resist to the last. The house would end up falling in on them, with all its cracks and dry rot. Not even the fact that they were willing to live more and more in the essential rooms (library, bedroom, dining room, kitchen), leaving the rest closed up, could save it from disaster. Moreover, Luisa was not the kind to give it the warmth of a home. She was home at the same time as he was, but it was as though they lived together in three impersonal hotel rooms. Every day she vacuumed off the dust, set the books back where they belonged, and put fresh flowers in the vases; but that invariable order was her way of establishing distance, of eliminating any glint of warmth or pleasantness. Her strangeness governed those three rooms; they underwent the same fluctuations as her moods. Moreover, there was something transitory in their lives and he knew it better than anyone, the sensation that this library was a kind of illuminated ship's bridge from which he observed a spectacle vast, monotonous, and threatening as the sea.

That spectacle, in the last few months, weighed too heavy on their lives, demanded a participation from them that was more and more irritating. It was no longer a matter of families divided and the thousands that had gone into exile, or those who waited in work camps for authorization to leave; it was an even greater weight—a feeling of being hunted which emanated from everything and was impossible to fight. He had drawn away from old friends, who resignedly accepted the change. He had distanced himself from his mother and his aunts, who finally left the country. He was attached only to Luisa and two or three friends who accepted his unpleasantness and his moodiness like a family evil and whose support and understanding made it possible for him to go on living in this situation, but from whom he knew he was growing more removed every day.

But the habit of solitude didn't bother him. He spent hours doing translations, having imaginary conversations with the authors, telling them with perfect frankness of his sympathy or disdain for their work. One day he would write something, too. He wouldn't be content just to translate other people's thoughts; he would express his own. But at the moment he didn't have the time. He had to resign himself to making furious notes in the margins of the pages he hastily translated so he could turn them in punctually every Friday.

One day, out of the blue, he would dedicate an entire night to Marcuse. It wasn't that he scorned him completely. *Eros and Civilization* was full of provocative ideas that could set off a turmoil of topics that had seemingly been gnawed to the bone in the last few years. *One-Dimensional Man* interested him less, and even less *The End of Utopia*, in which an aging spectator contemplates the way his theoretical model has been incarnated in groups of students erecting a Maoism of barricades, with no options but destruction and violence.

This man of seventy-odd years was going to have the last word, set the record straight. This old man in slippers (did he still make love?) spent hours proof-reading, correcting Karl Marx's galleys. Seemingly, he showed that the working class was no longer revolutionary, that it had gone over to the system, that its potential for revolution had been neutralized by the fetishism of a consumer society; the marginal social groups (he didn't dare call them classes) represented the greatest potential for action.

Now he would travel by plane, with that incomparable passport that opens all frontiers. Nationalized American, professor of the universities of abundance, he had written *Soviet Marxism* (that immanent analysis) while enjoying a Rockefeller grant to define a society, Russia's, whose most interesting feature, really, was its unknowns.

But he had formulated a theoretical schema and voilà! more than fifty years of struggle, stupidity, and greatness are compressed into a pile of precious observations whose cold balance leaves intact millions of corpses, the fuel of history.

Now he would be drinking a cup of tea with the circle of philosophers of the Frankfurt School. Horkheimer beside him, arguing. The U.S.S.R. was a verbal scheme; the Third World was a squeezed-out fruit, an approximate notion. But it was a day of tentative first winter; he ran, trembling with the cold. The German porter looked at him in surprise to see him mount the stairs in summer clothes like a vacationing student.

The first person he met was an elegant old man carrying several books under his arm. He asked him where the Frankfurt School met. The old man answered him in a neat accent, "There," and pointed out a door.

"Sartre isn't there, too?" he deferentially asked.

The old man slipped on the third step, did an elaborate balancing act to keep from falling, and looked at him as though Julio were mad.

He seemed annoyed. "My dear young man," he said haughtily, "that gentleman does not belong here," and turned away.

Julio felt humiliated. But he pulled himself together, attributing the man's behavior to old philosophical nationalisms, as rabid as any other, he assumed.

He decided to go to the door. He opened it and there was the group, staring at him in astonishment. Five old men were gathered at a table laden with sandwiches, open bottles, and every imaginable kind of cheese. He felt his stomach come alert; his eyes were fixed on the heaping lunch rather than on the group, which greeted his entrance with cordial good humor, as though he had come into the wrong hotel room and would have to back out, apologizing and bobbing his head.

They scrutinized him, an antelope come suddenly into the room, ready for the hunt. They howled with laughter, setting him apart, transfixing him, a bit of larva exposed to the keen scientific gaze of five observers.

There was a flurry of chairs and pinces-nez and the group surrounded him, pawing his clothes, pressing his chest. One of them put his ear over Julio's left breast pocket and shook his head, surprised that the heart was beating.

"I am . . ." he stammered, attempting to introduce himself.

Amazed at his syllables, they all laughed.

"Wonderful! The starting point for all ontology!" one of them shouted.

The others turned to the table, served themselves wine, devoured sandwiches, repeating his first words with the enthusiasm of novices.

He tried to explain. "I mean, I came from . . ."

And one of the old men put his finger to Julio's mouth, bringing to an end his incipient explanation. Julio heard his first seven words joined in a chant and repeated by the senile chorus like a rite of madness or magic: "I am, I mean, I came from . . ."

Three of them took him by the arms, propelled him from the back, and shoved him into a big armchair that sank soft under his weight. They crouched over him. A tiny old man, staring with intense blue eyes, passed him a platter. "Eat," he said. Trembling, his hand obeyed the order and he consumed sandwiches, glasses of wine, hunks of cheese. They observed him with a morose delectation, almost paternally. When the first spasms of hunger had subsided, he was embarrassed by his voracity. They seemed to guess that.

"Winter makes one hungry," said one.

"Which in the end is the only truly serious problem for philosophy," said another.

He said it looking at the man who from the first had acted as the thinking head of the group, the one to take the initiative.

"You, my dear fellow, are a bloody positivist," he said dryly. "Your only saving grace is that utopian star over your heart.

"Who sent you?" he asked, turning to Julio.

Julio recognized the voice of radio broadcasts and lectures, to which were added now the flesh-and-blood gestures of Professor Herbert Marcuse; it was the same authoritarian manner and tone. He stood looking out the window, through which came the sweet, penetrating fragrance of white night-blooming jasmine, and calculated that if he should have to make a leap for it, he would encounter no obstacle, and in fact at this hour could do it with complete impunity, for the students wouldn't be watching him.

"Because somebody sent you, there's no doubt about that."

"Günter," he replied.

"Günter? That's rich. He says Günter sent him." And they laughed again.

He took advantage of the disruption to hurl at them his entire notebook of accumulated objections.

. . .

From the bottom of his heart flowed ancient truths; no certainty, no theoretical model could withstand his withering words; the professors could not muster a single valid argument to pit against those flames and truths of his . . . They were all on their feet now, listening with fascinated attention, a grouping of figures from El Greco, elongated, fixed in the dramatic space of a stage on which the only really concrete thing was he, and the only really estimable opinions were his own; where he was now saying what for a long time had needed to be said, like St. Justin Martyr before a chorus of crackpots. Suddenly he took out a cigar (an H. Upman Número Uno) and brandished it like a spear. No one seemed capable of the slightest movement. He asked for a match. No one moved. He walked toward the group.

"You don't have a match?"

He repeated the question like a refrain. The old men began to pat their pockets in unison, methodically, as if obeying an order. He heard them slapping their pockets and heard their voices, which suddenly seemed to come from what had been the dining room of San Isidro, across the way, before Victoria Ocampo divided up the house, but in any case with the same nasal tones as José Bianco's.

"No, we don't have matches, but look how skinny we are! . . . how skinny we are! . . . how skinny we are! . . ."

"Matches!" Julio cried desperately. "What I need is a match!"

"Give that man a match!" he heard someone shout from the yard, from which arose the fragrance of the white night-blooming jasmine. And he saw that one of the rooms in the students' dormitory had a light on and some half-naked girls were watching the library, where he was gesturing, panting, the unlit cigar between his fingers.

"Julio." He heard Luisa's sleepy, alarmed voice.

He turned off the light. In the darkness he saw the girls laughing, coughing. Were they making fun of him?

"What's going on? Why are you shouting?"

"I was reading aloud, that's all."

"Why don't you go to bed? It's the middle of the night."

"I'm going to, right away."

"Bring me some water, please."

He went to the refrigerator and filled a glass. As he crossed the hall, he looked at himself in the mirror. He looked like a monk, with his white shirt hanging over his pants, his beard growing out, his eyes fevered, and the glass of water like a candlestick in his hand. "I look like a chinchilla. Ugly." And he made a face.

"Julio," Luisa called again.

"I'm coming."

The temperature of the bedroom was wonderful. The air conditioner hummed softly, displacing the hot fumes of summer.

"Hand me the Stelazine. I'm so tense. I've been having nightmares."

Luisa took the pills and washed them down with the water. She sat on the edge of the bed. He undressed and sat next to her. He saw himself in the dresser mirror, his naked torso, his face with its infantile features, in fact with the typical angry look of a child.

"You two spent the night arguing."

"A little," he said, and made her lie down.

"Did you clean out the ashtrays? I think I smell cigar smoke."

"I cleaned them all," he said.

Now he was looking at the ceiling, talking to her without looking at her. "All those water stains, and we can't paint them. It's awful."

"Don't worry about that," she said, wanting to sleep.

In a few moments he heard her deep, troubled breathing.

❦ 4 ❧

BUT SHE SPRANG UP suddenly, with her hair wild, and smelling of damp magnolias.

She walked along a beautiful ramp, on a remote hill, in another world, trying to keep her miniskirt down over her thighs, very happy. She whispered to him through her hands held like a megaphone, her voice hardly audible, as though she was telling him a secret, long-distance.

"The thing is solved."

"What?"

"It's solved."

"But what?" he insisted, trying to hear her.

"The thing, dummy, that's solved."

Then he saw her come, lovely and supple, along a road perfectly soft and gentle, so near him he didn't even have to stretch out his hand.

"You're coming with me right now," she said, taking him by the hand.

He obeyed, puzzled that for the first time he put up no resistance to her coaxing. She ruled the road, dodged obstacles like an expert. They crossed bright plains, ranches filled with animals, milk cows that looked at them with affecting, contented curiosity.

"There he is. Speak to him," she said, pointing to a man leaning against a ceiba tree, surrounded by officers, all of them smiling as though Julio's arrival had been expected.

He noticed a card table, and on it, stacks of papers arranged by date, place, subject, and person.

"Don't worry about that," Fidel said to him. "It's just routine. An unavoidable evil, you know—knowing what people are thinking and saying about you. For example, your case. That pile there." He pointed at the table, the stacks of files as high as walls. "You've talked a lot of bullshit, don't tell me you haven't. And what you've said about my *cows*—well, we'll talk about that later, another time, when there aren't so many people around."

"What I've said . . ." he timidly echoed.

Fidel came up to him and put his hand on his shoulder. He spoke softly, looking around to make sure he wasn't overheard. "Yes—that they have tuberculosis."

"I said that?"

"You repeated it, it's the same thing. But I don't want to talk about that now. They're lies spread by the CIA. I've taken personal charge of them and everybody knows that by '71 the problem will be what to do with all the milk. Didn't you see the ranches as you came? What possible doubt can you have that it's true? Because you certainly do doubt it. What kind are you—worm, wormoid, or big fat worm?"

"Me, Fidel . . ." he stammered.

"Yes, what kind? Because revolutionaries don't need to see me or talk to me. They have faith. And if you want to see me it's because you doubt. And whoever doubts is weak, soft, a worm. You think that I wasn't going to find out about your opinions? I know all of them. It's my duty. Well, what are you—worm, wormoid, or big fat worm?"

Julio just stared, watching the movement of Fidel's lips. The group imitated him, waiting to hear what he was going to say. Then he looked at Luisa, sitting on a rock, with her elbows on her joined knees and her chin on her hands, happy to see them finally face to face, her hair black and tangled and still holding that strange odor of damp magnolias. He looked, pleading, at her— but she gave him her usual sign of encouragement with her chin, as though pushing him along, urging him to tell his truth.

"Well, Fidel," he started to say, very slowly, "I think that I'm a critical intelligence." But his words left him empty, exposed, vulnerable.

Fidel blinked, as usual; he lowered and then raised his head, and turned to the group. "Did you hear that?"

They nodded.

"He's a critical intelligence," Fidel repeated in a loud voice, giving Julio's admission an almost bellicose heat, a sudden breath of sarcasm. He turned to the group for approval. "What category shall we put him in?"

The group huddled in a circle, each man with his arms around his neighbors' shoulders, and whispered among themselves. Then they turned toward the Chief as though expressing an unappealable verdict. "Intellectual," they said in unison.

Fidel smiled. He looked at Julio again. "Do you write?"

"I translate."

"But not privately."

Heberto Padilla

"No, no. For the government."

"For the *Revolution*," corrected Fidel. "Worms say for the government. Do you know what I think I'll do with you?" He began to pace back and forth, glancing slyly at Julio from time to time. "Do you know?" he asked again.

"No, Fidel, I don't know."

"Can't you guess?"

"Well, Fidel, I'd work anywhere."

"Are you sure?"

"Yes, Fidel, I'm sure."

With that, Fidel turned toward the group and pointed at Luisa. "Send her back. I'm leaving with this man," he said.

And Fidel started to march, huge, bearded, his breathing expansive.

A helicopter's blades began to turn, stirring the trees and grass. The stack of papers scattered on the ground.

"Don't worry." Fidel smiled. "That's trash."

The voice restored his confidence, gave him a new birth certificate in the world. He moved with spirit, full of pride and assurance. His clothes changed color; they glowed green, young. Now he could stand tall. He looked down through Fidel's binoculars, Fidel's hand on his shoulder, happier than a new father.

"Down there are my plans," Fidel told him. "Look at them. What do you have against them? There's rice, look."

The dark stain of plantings extended far out of sight.

"That's Camagüey. Juan Almeida, my right-hand man, and the boys are there. It's coming right along. And over there is San Andrés. There's the Centennial

Pillar. Over there was MUAP; you know all about that. It was bullshit, I admit." He leaned back in his seat, content with the enumeration of his projects. He looked at Julio for a long time. "But of course what really interests you are the laws, right?" Now he was looking grave.

"Yes, Fidel," Julio said, arming himself with anger. "Really, laws obsess me. The way I was educated, maybe."

"Don't talk to me about education, buddy. Do you think that five years of Roman law, business law, international law, and civil law is nothing? It's all bullshit. Forms, empty schemes."

"But a constitution doesn't seem necessary to you?"

"Why not? It'll be done."

"But it's been ten years already."

"What's ten years?"

"More than two presidential terms."

"You keep measuring life by the old patterns."

"Okay, more than two corrupt governments."

"That's better. Because, before, there were thieves. They existed even with constitutions and laws. What good were they to us?"

"But that doesn't invalidate their necessity."

"But it justifies the fact that we've postponed them, doesn't it?"

"Indefinitely, Fidel?"

"Blas Roca is working on that. There's a whole commission in the Party assigned to that. We don't want to rush it. It'll be done. What more do you want? Don't tell me you want general elections?"

"No, of course not."

[9 5]

"Well?"

"It seems to me the degree of participation of the masses in the decisions of the government . . ."

"Of the Revolution."

"No, in this case the revolutionary *government*."

". . . is insufficient, is that what you mean?"

"Yes."

"Do you think the mass meetings are nothing? Haven't we consulted the people, more than a million people gathered in the Plaza de la Revolución?"

"I think that's popular consensus, but it isn't the same as participation in decisions. Socialism means participating in decisions, Fidel."

Fidel fell back in his seat. He lit an H. Upman and blew out a huge puff of smoke. He nodded, all the while looking at Julio, and then threw a question at him. "And what would you do if you were Prime Minister? I'll give you one minute to answer. What would you do in my place?"

His eyes scrutinized him. Julio's intelligent, sick, old weight of objections froze before that compelling question, which admitted of no evasions. The answer burst out before he could stop it. "Exactly what you do, Fidel."

Fidel slapped him on the back. "That's just what I thought," he said. "What you are is a son of a bitch, a politician. I'm going to use you. There's not a speck of the intellectual in you."

He took a piece of paper and wrote something down. "Here," he said. "I've written what you must do."

Julio started to read it.

"No. Read it later. But read it carefully. One mistake and . . ." He slashed a finger across his throat.

Julio felt his head fly. Fidel smiled. He ordered the pilot to land. The ceiba tree was still there, the card table under it, the stack of papers and paper clips, with hens now pecking at them. Scattered there were the remnants of his telephone conversations, his sarcastic comments, his jokes, that sardonic mockery of his mordant personality—the symptoms of his sickness. He was free, returned to innocence, to a blank page on which his new steps, now resolute, solid, would be entered.

"Don't forget," Fidel said.

His escort closed around him again. Julio saw him walk away, affectionately patting the cows, stroking the calves, the country people smiling at him without taking their hands off the udders.

Julio was happy; he started to walk back along the road planted with orange trees and windbreaks. He whistled the army anthem, the *Internationale*, the Agrarian Reform hymn, the old melodies of the good years.

In spite of himself, he began to run. The road flew under his feet, the rocks flew past like wild doves. He stopped on the Quinta Avenida. He didn't want to seem too proud in his new happiness. He passed before Fernández Junco's house, trying to keep out of sight, since the old man was always ready to spill out his bile against the Revolution; but he was there, smoking in the garden, a few feet away.

"Julio!" he called out.

Julio waved.

"Hey," the old man said, louder. "I've got something to tell you. Come over here." He was smiling. "Didn't you hear?"

"What?"

"The guy that sells suckers, kid. He got his exit visa. He was with Fidel this afternoon."

Julio looked at him with an incredulous smile. "It can't be."

"Is the Pope Catholic? He got it today, and today Fidel put him on the plane."

"You're lying," said Julio with irritation.

Fernández Junco looked upset. "Well, okay, if you say so, I'm lying. Do you know why he got his visa?"

"I don't know anything."

"The other day he was in the plaza selling suckers. Fidel couldn't deliver his speech because the sucker man kept shouting 'Suckers! Suckers!' Imagine, Fidel got desperate. He had him brought up to him. The poor guy explained that he didn't have anything against the speech, he was just trying to make a living selling suckers. He had applied for an exit visa, but it hadn't come through. He told Fidel, right in front of everybody in the plaza. And you know what happened?"

Julio didn't answer.

Fernández lowered his voice. "Fidel called Immigration and said, 'Give that man an exit visa immediately!' And in a second the whole Plaza de la Revolución started chanting 'Suckers! Suckers!' "

The old man let out a guffaw. "You fell for it! I really got you! How do you like that joke?" The old man's huge belly was shaking. "Come on, brother! Nobody takes away this country's sense of humor! There's not a dictator that can conquer it . . ."

Julio looked at him indignantly and left him laughing in the enormous garden, patting the dog, who was jumping up and down beside him.

[98]

"I'll report him, goddamnit . . . I'll turn him in," he said aloud, and hurried away.

At the entrance to the regional office of the Party, a group of activists were talking in low voices, as though talking over one of their confidential directives. "One of *my* directives," he corrected himself. When he was a few steps away from them, he heard them say his name, and there was another slap on his back.

"Hello, Comrade Julio . . ."

He answered smugly, smiling at them.

On the corner of Calle 26 he felt bony fingers fasten themselves on his arm. It was the old woman Zaida, skinny, spindly, beautiful still, in spite of her imperious dark eyes.

"You know something?" she said.

"What?"

She put her fleshy lips to his ear. "It's really good; listen. She couldn't get into the Party."

"Who?"

Zaida began to laugh. "Santa Barbara. With a machete in her hand, and she's never cut a single stalk of cane." She let out a peal of laughter, watching him so she could enjoy the effect of the joke on Julio.

"Let me go," said Julio. "I'm in a hurry."

She followed, pulling at him.

"On the other hand, Our Lady of Charity . . ." she went on, laughing and coughing at the same time, "they already have her in the Federation. Imagine, with that tremendous boot of hers and she hasn't left the country . . ."

She grabbed him by the shoulders and shook him.

Julio pushed her away roughly. Zaida swayed on her high heels, sinuous and supple as a cat. She kept on tapping along behind him on her heels, skipping between the benches, making people laugh.

"I'll turn all these people in," he said to himself as he walked toward the house. Some students were picking up litter from the streets, piling it up and burning it. Julio watched them, meeting the open laughter of the boys and girls. He stooped, picked up some paper, and took it over to the little pyramid.

"Thank you, comrade," they chorused.

The president of the committee came out the door when he saw him go by. "Don't worry, Julio. 'Snothing. Scratch it out and start a new page."

"*Venceremos*," Julio responded.

And he went into his garden. "Tomorrow for sure I'm cutting all this grass. Maybe the students will help me. It would be good to organize a party for the poor kids. They're just little country boys. And they never see me but that I look like I'm going to a funeral, always groaning and depressed."

When he opened the door, he didn't waste a second. He sat down at the typewriter and began to write the first report. You had to give the revolutionary offensive a push, a real hand.

In a few minutes Zaida and Fernández Junco were perfectly delineated. "And with almost no adjectives, because we revolutionaries don't have to dramatize things unnecessarily. I have to tell about this continual sniping, the way these sons of bitches spread the little counterrevolutionary jokes they invent between games of canasta while they're living on Urban Reform assistance—but tell it plain. Just be straight. Let 'em get out whenever they want to, but if they're going to live here, they've got to keep their traps shut."

Suddenly his extremist fury began to worry him. Extremism was a perversion of natural impulses, and he knew it.

He worked the report over several times until he was sure he had suppressed all trace of resentment and accusation. When it was ready, he vaulted down the stairs. He went to the committee offices and handed the envelope to the president, who held it with emotion, winking at him like a conspirator. He went back home.

Through the library window he saw Luisa pacing with an open book, taking bites out of a piece of bread. He felt an intense affection in watching her.

In a second he had gone up the stairs, opened the door, and tried to grab Luisa's arm, but it gave him a glancing brush. Luisa began to wheel, light and transparent as tulle, her coppery skin grained with colors—greens, reds, browns, ochers—a Chagall. He leapt toward her and took a spill on the rug. He fell on his back; slowly, he opened his eyes. There were the water stains on the ceiling, the buzz of the air conditioner in his left ear, the long mirror reflecting him in profile, almost naked, with his growth of beard and those sleepy, absurdly happy eyes.

He sat up in bed and took a cigarette. He lighted it and inhaled several times. Luisa was in the kitchen. He heard her turn the water on and off, washing dishes in her fanatically thorough way. In a few minutes, she came in.

"You really slept," she said, and gave him a cup of coffee, which Julio drank eagerly.

"Cold," he said, handing her back the cup.

"It can't be."

"Cold."

"I don't understand. I just made it."

"It's cold anyway. It's always cold."

Luisa's eyes began to water.

"Don't get dramatic, please."

"Everything I do is wrong."

"I'm talking about coffee."

"Everything, Julio. You don't like anything I do. You always find something wrong."

She was sobbing. Julio took her by the arm and made her sit down.

"Leave me alone," she said. "I'm so nervous and all you ever do is bug me."

He began to rain kisses all over her body and they fell onto the bed. They stayed there a long while, breathing in unison.

"You know I had a dream?" he began to tell her.

"It's been a long time since I had a dream," she said.

"An incredible dream. It bothers me even to tell it," he said.

"Me, I haven't dreamed in a long time."

"Dreams are wonderful," he said.

She sat up on the side of the bed. "You know what I used to dream about when I was a girl?"

"No. Animals, I guess. Wild animals. It's very common."

"Sometimes, yes; but especially about a bridge. I'd start walking on it and the bridge would fall. It was like an obsession."

He stood up and went into the bathroom. "I dreamed about you, too," he said as he turned on the taps, snorting as he washed his face.

She lay down on the bed. "You have to tell me about it sometime."

He was at the bathroom door, drying himself off. "I'd like to know exactly what the mechanism of dreams is, because I just don't agree with Freud," he said.

"What about Jung?"

"Even less. He was an old table-rapper."

"I think a lot of dreams come true."

"Don't be ridiculous."

"What was I doing in your dream?"

"I dreamed I had a meeting with Fidel," he said, smiling.

"Did you manage to kill him?" she joked.

"Quite the contrary. We became great friends."

"Freud says that's what you want to happen."

"I argued with him. You had taken me to see him. I told him what I thought, everything. Dreams are incredible."

He started to get dressed.

"Aren't you hungry?"

"Yes, I'm starved."

"Well, get dressed, because I have a surprise."

She ran to the kitchen and he heard her bustling around for several minutes. She reappeared and led him by the arm to the table and began to take the covers off several platters. "There you go—an omelet with lots of onions. Coffee, toast . . ."

They sat down and began to devour the food.

Summer was ending, the most enervating part of summer. He could detect the slightest changes of temperature as he breathed, in the wings of his nose. The air began to grow thinner, the hot summer fumes didn't hang in the air as before, the fragrance of foliage which came in from the garden left a sharp, heady flavor on his palate. The endless days of summer that made the asphalt shimmer and raised a trembling light from the earth seemed finally to soften—those stifling days (90 percent humidity), everyone crowded together at the bus stops under the few dried-out trees, which scarcely gave any shade; women holding ratty old parasols over themselves, or scraps of newspapers, or handbags, some of them seeking relief by standing in the thin line of shadow thrown by lampposts. That was the disgusting, persistently humid island summer he had hated since he had had the use of reason, when the huge flat sea of the bay withheld all possibility of coolness, in fact burned like a refracting mirror, doubling the intensity of the sun, and flung its stinging salt against the pillars and façades of buildings, the faces of the islanders—devouring them, wrinkling and aging the skin prematurely. He hated that sun, the humiliating reverse of snow.

"The day they start a revolution against this climate, I'll be the first martyr," he said, coming out of the refrigerated bedroom.

"Well, you know its laws. You'll know when to set off the first bomb."

"In August."

"Why? The inferno begins at the end of May."

"But if I set off a fragmentation bomb in August, I'll get all the months around it, and it won't do anything to the winter."

"A pretty precarious winter, at that."

"But tolerable. I like winter in Cuba. It's an aberration. No snow, green leaves, and you can swim in the ocean. Can you imagine?"

He went back into the air conditioning as though into a bomb shelter. He looked out of the window toward the bus stop, an infernal aquarium. He called Luisa. "Look at them. They look like fish. They've been about to fry themselves in oil this summer. It's like Dante."

Luisa looked at him, laughing. "You're crazy as hell, Julio. You should have gone on living in Europe. There you'd have your four seasons."

He threw himself on the bed and stared at the ceiling. "My four seasons," he said, absorbed. "My four inns, my four crowded trains, my four trees, my four fig trees, my four old boots, my four sparrows, my four gray ladies, my four bridges, my four Bach fugues."

"Julio!" she cried.

"My four streaming flags . . ."

"Stop, Julio . . ."

"My four lucky traders, my four gentle mornings, my four joys."

"And your four illnesses and your four daily insulin shots and your four electroshocks."

Now he was staring at her. "I'm kidding, shit, but I'll tell you, there are four seasons—which you've seen only in photographs but I've felt on my skin, on my ears, on my tongue, on my eyes."

"I don't envy you any of that. *I've* got you now."

"That's what you think," he said in a low voice.

"You'll never leave me. Have no illusions about that."

"One day I'll get on a ship, or even a little boat if there's no other way."

"I'll come to the jail to see you. The coast guard will grab you."

He started to put on his tie.

"What are you doing?"

"I can report to you that the climate has changed. I feel it in the wings of my nose. So long, dear summer, you ugly clown!"

She laughed aloud.

"Change your expression. Because you're going to have to dry a lot of tears." He knotted his tie before the mirror. "I'll send you a telegram from London."

"There's no work camp by that name," said Luisa, laughing again.

"Of course there is. It's called Soho, and better yet, it's a jungle."

"A camp for aristocrats, you mean."

"For aristocrats. How little you know."

"They would ride horses through the fields, yelling 'Soooohooo . . .' That's where the name comes from. I read that."

He took her by the hair and pulled it.

"Brute," she said to him.

"I'd like to jam a Cossack cap on your head."

"Leave me alone."

"You'd look very tough. A kind of classy homosexual. A fag Cossack with big sweet eyes, very, very black. A good museum piece."

She watched him, penned and defenseless. "You're an infernal machine, Julio."

"I don't hurt anybody."

"You hurt more than you can imagine," she said in a low voice. "You threaten me. You describe me as a ridiculous Cossack. You want to leave me."

He put on his jacket without replying.

"Where are you going?"

"I'll be right back. I'm going to turn in the translation."

"Take me with you."

"If Günter comes, tell him I'll be back in an hour."

"Why don't you take me. I can get dressed in a second."

Hurriedly, she began to undress and was instantly naked. She went to the closet and took out a dress. He looked at her from the front, the back, in profile. I wonder how many men have seen her like that, he thought. How many men has she really gone to bed with? She walks around stark naked. There are women who don't. Who turn off the lights to make love. She'd like a spotlight. She's theatrical. She likes to excite me, to show herself off, likes me to see her. To show it all to me. But if she thinks she's got me, she's very fucking mistaken. One day I'm leaving. One day when she least expects it. You'll have to look for me a long way off, little hoyden.

Luisa started to dress.

"I'm going," he said.

He went to the library and got some cigars. He stuffed them into his jacket pocket. He heeded the gestures of the three men in the painting and lowered his head, creeping along cautiously so the branches of the mangrove didn't make the least rustle.

"Will you drop me off at the Ministry?"

He put a hand on the edge and vaulted. The bottom of the boat creaked.

"Aren't you going to take me?"

He began to row. The boat pulled away under the

impulse of his oars. The coastline was a dark stain on the gray waters.

"Look. I'm ready."

She was beside him, admirably dressed in blue, her hair held back with a ribbon like a teenager's, without makeup, her big sparkling eyes fixed on him.

5

OBVIOUSLY, the climate had changed. Luisa admitted it when they got into the car. Sitting next to her, gripping the steering wheel with the vehemence he had put into driving lately (and which he took conscious pleasure in), Julio glanced at her and with one hand caressed her hair, and flung himself into her rambling daydream—live another life, in another place, in any country at all, rent an apartment. They only needed to buy a newspaper to do that, and they could pick out the neighborhood, the size and rent of the place, anywhere in Europe or the Americas—better the Americas, he was repelled by so much old Europe, stupefied by the false fires of hope. They would sit everybody down and tell 'em, the idiots! those caravans of dreamers prowling about hotels. No, he no longer wanted to live again in Paris or London; the venom came from there. Instead, give him exotic, parodic places, like Argentina, for example, or Uruguay. He would set up an early-warning-system office there, not warning of terrorists or generals (which are only a kind of temporary fodder for the hemisphere, anyway), but rather warning of stupid serious men. He knew the perfect formula for detecting the grotesque alloy from which petty tyrants and novelists are formed.

"Isn't that right, Luisa?"

She laughed. "Absolutely. We're sailors, and we sail the seas, as Mr. Coleridge might have said."

The day was splendid, no doubt about it. It was pleasant to move under that sky toward the sea a little burnished and totally blue—Julio decided to declare that he was happy. Happy.

"I wish you said that oftener."

"And I shall. I'll tell you oftener, much oftener."

He looked at her with that happiness, a bit irrational, lost, which she most feared. But the last part of the trip left them smiling. She began to sing "Let It Be" and he swore that that was a fucking protest song, and she sang another one and he said the songs of the Party were much more solid.

He stopped the car in front of the Ministry. "Will you be able to push your project through today?" he called out, kidding her.

"At least I'll exhaust the realm of the possible, as Pascal Pindar says."

"So long, hoyden."

In a little while he scarcely saw her, a blue dot waving tiny in the rearview mirror.

He headed for the Hotel Nacional. Ona would be prowling around, somewhere in the hotel, and the first place that occurred to him was the pool. Tourists feel an almost morbid exaltation in exposing their milky, goosebumpy skin to the sun of the tropics. In a very few hours their skin, weathered in a different way by the long merciless winter, acquires the reddish tint of Gulf lobsters; their eyes, usually blue, sparkle on stinging cheeks. This was the gold that Cuba could openhandedly bestow.

In the lobby of the hotel he saw Günter, who was saying goodbye to a very thin black girl. It was Ara, one of the many girls Günter picked up at random on buses. Günter was always prepared with a card with his name and telephone number on it, and every time he ran into an attractive black girl, he would give her a card. He had better than a twenty percent rate of success. Julio had never known a foreigner to pick up so quickly on the psychology of a country. He was twenty-three years old, tall, corpulent, with blond, straight, thinning hair, his skin very white, and he had the smiling face of a child. He had a passion for the Frankfurt School, and kept up a correspondence with the survivors and their acolytes; he himself had been a student of Leo Kofler. He had deserted from the German army for political reasons and had come to Cuba as a political refugee. He was one of Dutschke's group, a passionate militant of the German New Left, but Marxism for him was a critical theory, nothing more.

When Ara had gone, Günter came to greet him. He was very nervous; he took him off to one side and spoke in a whisper, looking around cautiously. "Have you heard?"

Julio stared uncomprehendingly at him.

"Nobody has told you anything? I went to your house to see you. They threw me out of the country. Tomorrow I have to get out. And take my word for it, too, we're superwatched. I can assure you that they're watching us right now—maybe listening. It'll probably be better if we go out back to the garden."

They walked toward the wide garden set on the cliff

that ran to the edge of the sea. They had come to look for Günter that morning, to his own rooms. They showed him the expulsion order, "as an undesirable," signed by the Minister of the Interior; they submitted him to a long interrogation in which Julio's name had figured more than once. "They know your 'life and miracles,' everything about you." He was sweating but made an effort to be coherent.

"Try to get hold of yourself a little."

"I can't, I can't," Günter exclaimed. "I can't think logically. What the fuck are you doing with a woman's suitcase?"

Julio explained.

"Then we can't talk?"

"But can't it be later?" Julio said.

Günter had to settle his hotel bill. And he didn't know what to do with the bushels of books in his room. Why didn't Julio keep them? They were all German. Julio said he could see him at six, and anyway Günter couldn't leave the hotel.

Günter asked him to call his room as soon as he was finished with the Swedish girl. "But—what do you think about what I've told you?"

"We'll talk later," Julio said.

"Don't forget, Julio, I'll be waiting for you to call," Günter insisted.

"As soon as I'm finished with the Swedish girl, I'll give you a ring and you can come down."

He recognized her immediately at the other end of the swimming pool. She was wearing a dark blue bathing suit that emphasized her trim body. She advanced with long steps to the end of the diving board. She bent, her arms tense and her hands thrown behind her, and leapt. He knew she had seen him from the first, because she waved a hand in his direction the instant she emerged. He waved back. Seconds later she swam up to the edge of the pool in elegant strokes.

"Hi."

She tossed back her golden, dripping hair. Her shoulders and cheeks were a little sunburned and she smiled openly; but there was something of other latitudes in her face, perhaps a puzzled, slightly innocent air to her eyes or the way her lips, too young for her age, barely covered her large white teeth. She was not exactly beautiful.

"Oh, I hadn't missed it," she said, looking at the bag.

"I wanted to bring it last night, but the hotel assured me there was no one here by that name."

"You have a nice country here, Julio. They take all sorts of precautions."

"Shall we go up?"

She untied the room key from the strap of her bathing suit and handed the key to him. She explained that the elevator operator had strict instructions not to allow anyone who wasn't a guest to enter.

"How did you find that out?"

"At breakfast time. There's a kind of grapevine among the guests. I know a lot of other things; I invite you to a little complicity. Don't you like these little illicit situations? Now, in Europe, being a scofflaw has an enchanting subversiveness about it. People feel a little like guerrillas in all that decorousness." She smiled naughtily. "I suppose I'll change in Cuba. In the three weeks I'll be here, I'll become another woman—at least a little different, don't you think?"

Julio said her defiance of hotel discipline would defeat her purpose. She laughed enthusiastically.

They entered the elevator with a loud group of Russians and Czechs who were also returning from the pool, so his fear of being caught red-handed with another person's room key turned out to be completely wasted emotion. The elevator operator didn't even notice them. He asked for the floor number.

In the hotel room, while she dried her hair, Ona was still laughing. "You see how easy it would be to show a skeptic that Cuba isn't a police state! Though the way they do certain things *is* like Eastern Europe. Anyway, now I have an accomplice." She aimed her index finger at him. "Don't you like being my accomplice?"

He looked directly into her eyes, which prolonged the game. "Why not? I hope it has its advantages."

"There you are; I trust that you'll know how to appreciate them as much as I do"—she indicated the bottles of good Caney rum lined up in the cases from CIIF. "Help yourself while I shower. Then I want to ask you for some advice. I warn you I'm going to take full advantage of you."

Julio looked at her seriously for a few moments, but he met a neutral gaze.

"Later we'll go down to get something to eat; if there's time, of course."

She went into the bath and turned on the water. Julio poured himself a little of the fine mellow rum. He drank it down in one swallow. In the open suitcases there were more magazines, newspapers, and papers than

clothes. He sat down in one of the chairs and contemplated the hotel room. He drank some more Caney.

After a little while he heard Ona's voice. "There's a
dress in the blue suitcase on the bed. Will you hand it
to me?"

A while later, in the dining room, Julio spoke to her
of Sweden. He told her he had lived in Sundbyberg;
he'd enjoyed making the trip to Stockholm daily, especially in wintertime. The cemetery was beautiful, too;
the bus passed just a few yards from it, so you could see
Strindberg's tomb among the headstones covered with
snow except under the blackish tree trunks. The Swedes
had impressed him. In spite of the structure of the city,
which had so much of the impersonality of American
cities, it was in good taste. The buildings were almost
ascetic, with simple lines quite unlike the tin baroque
you saw in Yankee cities. Swedish comfort was not
excessive. And in Stockholm you could still drink coffee
and have a long conversation over an empty cup, and
not have the waiter hovering with that urging solicitude
that makes it clear he'd like you to leave the place free
for someone else. He said he admired the interest the
Swedes take in world problems—he claimed he'd seen
more international news stories on Swedish television
than in all the newsreels in the world.

He was still going on enthusiastically about Sweden
when Ona interrupted him, smiling. "You know, Julio?
I'm not really Swedish."

That was a surprise.

"I mean, I wasn't born there; I was born in Hungary.
They took me to Finland when I was a very little girl;

when I was five, I went to Sweden. My father used to say all the time, 'Small countries are small countries,' and even though the Finns make the Swedes out to be imperialists, in Sweden there was country, security, future."

"I like Finland," said Julio.

"I do too, a lot. My father never would have left Helsinki, but—" Her voice became hoarse, guttural. " 'Sweden is Sweden,' he would say. We lived for a long time in Göteborg, and two years in Malmö. My father would go to Copenhagen to give lectures. A lot of times I went with him. We'd get into his Saab and cross the ocean on the ferry. But later my father said Stockholm was Stockholm, the capital was the capital, and so on, *ad infinitum*."

She laughed. But suddenly she took on a sad, grave air. "He died in misery. I mean, practically in misery."

Then she turned to Julio and spoke dramatically. "So, my dear Cuban, from these miseries and all that to-ing and fro-ing was born what you see here before you—a bundle of nerves and furor." She laughed once more. "Does that sound like Ibsen? Isn't he like that? It's Scandinavia—the ballads, the tales of witches, the forests. When I was a girl, I recited in school. The boys liked the way I recited from *Peer Gynt*. For them, any Hungarian had something of the gypsy about her, and then these eyes"—and she opened them wide—"these eyes seemed very appropriate to them—black eyes, incredible in Scandinavia. 'Where do you take me, coachman of devils?' I'd shout, and the little boys would listen, amazed. The teachers, too. They thought I was going to be an actress. And you see—I've grown up to be a sociologist. I still have history. What has to be done.

What you've done here. Cuba! what a feat! Tell me, Julio, without modesty, doesn't it seem a great feat to you?"

He nodded. Undoubtedly, it was a great feat.

"And ninety miles away," she exclaimed, astonished, "ninety miles away there's a Yankee military base! You are a people truly young."

Julio observed her without speaking.

"Don't you think so?" Ona insisted.

He said then that he didn't believe in young peoples.

"Well," she said, "I mean countries that haven't entered history."

"But that gives them no right to youth. If they haven't made what you call history, it's because they've been marginalized."

"They've struggled, of course, but I'm talking about history itself, its core. Now is different."

"Miserable countries don't make history until they've been liberated; what you call ahistoricity . . ."

"I didn't say that," she interrupted.

"Okay, prehistoricity. It's the same thing; long neglect makes countries old. It makes them older than anything, the way misery makes adults of children. Maturity has its natural course. The rest is a snap."

"Snap," she said. "Pretty word. How do you say that in Spanish?"

He translated for her. "*Chasquido.*"

"You accuse me of thinking in schematics. It's true. The time has come for you, in the New World, to teach me."

"Europe can still teach, Europe is the only thing that can really teach," he said.

"Now it's you who are making use of schemas."

[1 1 7]

"You're mistaken," Julio said. "It's what I truly think."

"You say Europe, but what about Asia? Isn't it giving us a lesson? A world of hundreds of millions of inhabitants is waking up there."

"But that awakening has nothing to do with Europe."

"Oh, yes, it does," she said. "It has everything to do with Europe, everything."

"For instance, a cultural revolution in France, in Great Britain—do you consider that natural, organic?"

"In the literal sense, no, but there is a way in which, somehow, it would be a lesson. An old servitude, a secular misery which would be eradicated in fifteen years. We, in order to make a change, even the slightest change, in our university curricula, have to have martyrs. Any change at all makes our hair stand on end. You see what happened in Paris. And those were merely student demands. In Germany, such a thing can't even be imagined. They killed two of our comrades, in commune number 3. The police."

"Commune number 3?"

"Well, the last one. I was in number 2. But that was a nest of myopic dreamers and cowards. The only thing they thought about was sex. Sex, well, sex; but sex, only sex, who can be interested? Once I asked Peter about Vietnam. He said, getting very stuffy, 'I've got enough problems with my orgasm.' Can you imagine?"

This time he looked into her eyes with open desire. Well stocked with ideological fire, tenacious, handsome, at once intelligent and stupid, enveloped in a simple blue dress, and defiant almost by nature, she brought a strange tenderness to every one of her observations. Twenty-two at most. Her long, elegant neck was tanned by the sun. In the gold triangle below her throat he could imagine the breasts, the taut length of young skin enclosing her from head to foot, that smooth, flawless, young frame of health. By the time he was thirty he had already discovered the almost invisible stigmata of death —tiny red dots on his chest, minute cysts that were like excrescences of his skin.

"Can you imagine?" Ona insisted. But he didn't reply; he went on gazing at her. She sat so still that he brushed her hair back, placed his palms on her golden cheeks, kissed her until she could hardly breathe. All this golden nakedness, save in the virgin area covered by her minimal two-piece bathing suit; the father, self-denying, weary, strained to the breaking point, trying to get through the terrible postwar rationing (he would have been Julio's age at the time), bringing home the food that this creature, who would later give herself to the obscene promiscuity of males, needed to grow—honeycomb, warm fresh milk, fruit, lamb, all the air, all the winters, all the lovely suns of the Hungarian vintage laboring to produce a girl, a teenage girl. Now his dead contemporary was just a somewhat critical, somewhat pious quotation by the spindly daughter. The sacred balls, the sacred phallus which Herr Freud had so greatly exalted culminated in this girl, who had come thousands of miles in search of hope, from the very place where millions had struggled and died since 1968 to make it come true.

"I can imagine, yes," said Julio finally.

In Finland (how old *was* she, he wondered), later in Sweden—her father, fiftyish, prey no doubt to the first intimations of death, being bent as she straightened from his utmost efforts. The conclusion was simple: "He died

in misery." Ona had said that to him gravely, unconscious of the humiliating immorality that survival
implies to struggling people. So Julio knelt before the
grave, surely covered with snow and flowers, and felt that
the man lying in it saw him and smiled and said, "I
leave this body to the world; I will live in the complex
orgasm of this woman."

"How old were you when your father died?"

"Twelve."

"And him, how old was he when he died?"

"Fairly young, fifty-three."

"You haven't told me anything about your mother."

"I know very little about her; the war swallowed her
up, as it did so many. She tried, but she just wasn't able
to survive that experience. She always had nightmares—
bombings, sirens. We had a photograph in the house,
with flowers. I vaguely remember her, very vaguely,
really; but it's a memory of love. My father loved her
very much, they had been happy when they were young
together. He could never marry again. He devoted himself entirely to me. He worked very hard so I would be
able to study—to pay the tuition and board at the
university. I always went to private schools. To make a
long story short, I graduated and left for Berlin, where
I met a bunch of shortsighted dreamers who preached
liberation and equality but had the most terrible notion
of women. We're no more than dishrags to them. That's
why Cuba interests me so much; here women participate
on a par with men; they're real companions, comrades.
You know, that's one of the few words in Spanish that's
really beautiful to me—*compañera*. And what about
you, Julio—are you married? Don't tell me. I know
you're married. Besides being a sociologist at the univer-

sity, I'm told I have certain powers—what shall I say?—
the powers of a seer. They said I was one of those
Hungarian women who hang around train platforms in
Budapest and can tell you the day and hour of your
death."

She smiled mischievously, took a glass of water in her
hands, and turned it slowly.

"Married, of course. Still no children, though you will
have—you have—a happy marriage. You are not, and
that pleases me, one of those gross machos European
propaganda thinks of as the symbol of Latin culture.
Now, have I got it or not?"

"Not exactly."

"Then you have children."

"No."

At that moment a group of tourists burst into the pool,
noisily flaunting their delight. People of a certain age.
Security agents moved among them as though on a
chessboard. He could feel their gaze on his back.

"Everyone finds happiness in your country, Julio."

She affectionately observed the group as waiters attended to them with solicitude. Informants, thought
Julio; otherwise they couldn't work here.

The tourists were French or Italian, the first always
to bestow contempt or admiration on revolutionary
movements. Only after they give their okay does a wave
of Swedes and Germans come in. The daiquiri glasses
were emptied and refilled.

Borne in by the sea and utterly unconscious of displaying their countries' "fashions," they seemed to Julio
to be garbed in the unmistakable uniform of the
serious-foolish. Disillusioned by the arthritic socialist
experiences of Europe, they imagined they had found

spontaneity here in a budding revolution. They gave no thought to the legal system. What had the U.S.S.R. and Eastern Europe taught them? Down with bureaucracies! Government in the streets! Let the people participate directly in decision-making! This was what most excited them. The great, typically European happiness. It didn't occur to them that the absence of a parliament didn't mean governing in the streets, didn't eliminate coercion by the state, which still existed, and quite forcibly, in all its possible aspects, under the orders of a single authoritarian head.

These travelers liked to show themselves in the living flesh. Their countries could only contribute technique, technology, not moral alternatives. They could not give aid to Cuba on its own terms. They delivered themselves up to exoticism, their self-criticism making any thought of suicide impossible. Every revolution, however remote, personified for them the ideals which their nations lacked.

The more *barbarie* those distant revolutions exhibit, the more numerous the sympathizers and adepts. Pro-Chinese! Pro-Cuban! Accepting all the monstrousness these Europeans find reprehensible in their own nations. This was the culmination of a decadent attitude which mixed fatuous ingenuousness with the most abject nihilism, all under the rubric of "understanding." But he knew, had known for years, that this understanding is nothing but rationalization, and all rationalization a form of complicity. He distrusted the fond hope of these beautiful, enthusiastic souls who descend on the precarious countries of the Third World and later return to their comfortable cities with four hundred or so pages about that world, pages written in ignorance or even falsified, in the name of hope.

They carry the toxin within them, passion in anticipation, love for charismatics. It never occurred to them that charismatics are essentially gamblers who love the rules of the game to the point of delirium and can't bear for anyone to oppose them. If anyone dares to, such men do away with established convention, substituting the rudimentary decalogue of their whims, which the country then suffers under. Men whom sociology can't deal with, as Max Weber tried to; they belong to the annals of clinical psychology or criminology, not to sociology. The will to power, which Nietzsche situated at the core of human nature, cannot be satisfied just by prevailing or submitting. In every act of terror there is a desperate desire to persuade. Had it not been said that shooting at random into a crowd was an expression of frantic love? That was mere conjecture when it was said; history had not yet made it real. Did tyrants love their countries —that was the question. He thought they did, with the darkest, most jealous and constant love. What the failure of a five-year plan meant to Stalin's heart, no one could fathom. The order to fire into a starving crowd demanding bread is a form of ecstatic love. Though the crowd judge it monstrous, it is not hatred. There is a deep, loving, relentless poignancy in it. Technically, tyranny is only an option, a choice the governing party makes, and not always the ultimate one. No one has ever analyzed tyranny from the point of view of the tyrant. Science is too full of ethics, of diffuse theology, to undertake such an analysis. If Adorno proposed an analysis of history from the point of view of the defeated, why not from the point of view of the tyrant? All public hands are stained with blood; the tyrant's are simply two hands more. At what moment of history had the will to suppress terror really eliminated it? Years of guillotining have not improved mankind; men go on killing each other. In every criminal's mind there is always the certainty of an invulnerable expertise, of an infallible alibi. When he shoots, stabs, or poisons, he does not foresee the gas chamber, the gallows, the scaffold.

On more than one occasion, Julio had expounded on these ideas to Humberto; Humberto had simply categorized him as a skeptic. He wanted, of course, to call him, at the very least, a pessimist. Curious how, in time, words become synonymous. Nothing farther, though, from the pretensions of Pyrrho or the Sixth Empire. Empire—from there had come the epithet "empiricism," induction in a savage state, paving a broad way for John Stuart Mill and Bacon, asking of us only that we attend to appearances. If honey is not sweet, let us at least give importance to the fact that it seems to be. What is important are its symptoms, its signs. Instinct is the best counselor, and as it proposed happiness, imperturbability, the state in which nothing upsets or anguishes us, it likewise counseled the acceptance of laws, usages, and customs—including, of course, institutions and even religions. None of his friends knew that skeptics were the flagbearers of a *happy* philosophy, as Alfonso Reyes said.

Cynic, fanatic, or skeptic, he, Julio, delighted in, was proud of, his lucid enthusiasm.

He had nothing to say to these visitors. Faded youth looked out from the faces of the women—poor cats bereft of the pleasures of eroticism or tenderness, accompanied by cordial, understanding husbands, in the depth of whose eyes, however, there were remnants of a morbid disillusionment that not even the tropics could dissipate.

And here they all were, disporting themselves, followed by the guides from the Institute for International Friendship, who passed out sombreros and flags, emblems of the gaiety of the occasion.

Julio thought of the thousands of cane cutters who at that very moment were longing desperately to fall into their hammocks, to gulp down a handful of rice and beans, every day's sad end to their work.

"Well, we have to get on with your next activity. I'm at your service."

"Everything, everything interests me!" Ona exclaimed warmly, her voice rising above the enthusiasm at the pool. Several tourists sitting at nearby tables turned in curiosity.

"Do you need me tonight?" Julio asked.

"No, thanks. What with the trip and the hours in the pool, I'm exhausted. Anyway, I'll map out an itinerary tonight and we'll discuss it tomorrow. Is that all right with you?"

When he left Ona, he called Günter, who answered on the first ring. A little later Günter stepped out of the elevator, paler and more anxious than before.

"We'd better talk in the garden. They're after me."

"After everybody, kiddo," Julio said.

"Hah! If you only knew!"

The garden was almost deserted. The ocean beat more strongly now and the afternoon was growing cooler. A mist of salt spray hung over them. They sat on one of the benches, from which they could observe any movement around them. But Julio knew that behind the most insignificant object, in the bushes or from above, from those rooms that opened out onto the ocean, eyes might be spying, ears listening.

Günter told him about the three armed men who spoke with such anger. Cuba thought it had taken in a young German leftist, a real revolutionary, but he spent his time hunting out black women in the streets and hanging around with all the bitter pseudo-intellectuals in the country, running down Cuban politics. They were enemies of the radicalization of Cuba. They wanted to be taken for honest critics, but all they did was spew venom in the hotels, among the tourists. "You're a piece of shit, mister," said one of the men, displaying a pistol. "And you can thank the generosity of the Revolution that we don't throw you head-first into jail, because there are more than enough reasons to do it. Under cover of your 'sociology,' you trail after every resentful black in the street. What they think and say interests you, so later they can show up in one of those scientific little books of yours. Well, listen, write anything you like! It's no sweat off the balls of the Cuban Revolution! And let me tell you that we know all about you. And if we haven't caught you with a rod up your ass, it's because we haven't wanted to. Because you're a fag, you hear me. That's what you are. Just like your friend Julio. We know what you two talk about, even if you speak German. We have more than enough qualified staff who speak every language. That Julio better watch out ..."

The man spoke with incredible fury, and it was clear that he was high-ranking. Günter was told to have everything ready for that very night. Other comrades would take him to the airport. They ordered him not to telephone anyone.

"Our meeting was a stroke of luck—I'm glad you came. What do you think of all this?" Günter asked. "What's going to happen to this country?"

"What's already happening, you mean. They're persecuting anyone with an opinion. They want to make opinions a crime."

"Shit!" Günter exclaimed. "That would be the end. It might come down then to a fight between factions for the leadership."

Julio interrupted. If Günter didn't want to wind up on his butt in jail, as the agent had warned him, he shouldn't look for political explanations for the incident. The version they gave him, of himself as predator of black women, was the best.

"But what about Ara? What will happen to her?"

"She'll take *cAra* herself," said Julio, stressing the pun in irritation.

Tears came to Günter's eyes. "You know, I really love her."

"You haven't been good for her at all. They'll simply try to blackmail her, or if not, maybe suggest she should . . ."

"Don't screw around, Julio. It wasn't like that. Ara wouldn't let herself be put in the position of being an informant for those people—she hates them. *You* see police everywhere."

"I see them, but they see *you*, and throw you out."

"Cubans can never be serious. Not even you."

Julio smiled bitterly. Günter was right. Cubans find in humor, in joking, the only way of defending themselves against any terrible situation. The Cuban becomes tragic only in madness. His only really serious contact with reality is at the moment he loses his identity.

"What will happen to you?"

"For the moment, I have to pick up the Swedish girl, who is certainly not Swedish, she's a living anthology of countries—and take her who knows where. So the possibility still exists that we'll see each other tomorrow."

"They're coming to get me tonight. I already told you."

"They could come to get me, too. The same odds that you won't leave tonight apply to my coming to the hotel tomorrow morning."

Günter was silent for a few seconds. Then he said, "I'll figure you out yet, Julio. I'll have a lot of time to think about this experience. I hope it won't end here," he added, smiling sadly, "and don't lose your exuberance, goddamnit."

It was his favorite word. He used it as his most powerful ejaculation during the long political arguments with Julio. Günter would wait with special interest for the moment when theory and practice overlapped; Julio would pile on contradictions and exceptions. And though the German thought he could climb aboard the Cuban movement with his personal theoretical baggage, sometimes he could not hide his failure: "It's curious that, as bright as this country is, it's so damn murky. You can't get a firm hold on anything!"

Julio left the hotel certain that he would never see Günter again, and hurried to the car; any moment, an arm might detain him. That's how they acted, by surprise, to make the strongest statement possible about authority. In a little while, however, he decided no one was following him, so he began to act naturally. He had never driven the car with such indifference, nor did he hurry to get it in the garage, as he opened and closed the iron gates, or look to see if the light in the library was on or off. Günter put an end to a stage in his life, and perhaps his expulsion would lend calm to another one.

He recounted the scene to Luisa, omitting the part that concerned himself, and she speculated over the incident with such clearsightedness that it was as though she had been there.

"I'm afraid, Julio."

All night, she tossed and turned in bed, struggling for the sleep that he couldn't find either.

Hours later, both gave in to exhaustion and sank without realizing it into sleep. When he awoke, he saw that Luisa was still asleep beside him. He thought Günter was probably about to land in some cold airport in Europe. It was very early; through the shutters, the dawn's light was still very faint. He got up, trying not to wake Luisa, and looked carefully toward the street. He saw no one—not even in the student lodgings was there any movement. But in Gregorio's house a light was burning, and Gloria's shadow was gliding slowly through the bedroom; she must be giving the baby his milk.

He took the one-cup Italian coffeemaker and made coffee, with surprising relief. The night had dissolved the anxieties of the evening before; he found a happy novelty in this routine act. Even the sunrise seemed different to him, even the solitude he sometimes felt locked inside of. He told himself he had never counted his blessings as he should have. Instead of letting himself be obsessed by history and social problems, instead of giving way to unconfessed but very real irritation toward those he considered inferior (the irritation of the unjustly marginalized man), instead of constantly theorizing, he should appreciate what he had—a tranquil existence with Luisa, a handful of friends who helped and were loyal to him beyond the call of duty. Or perhaps he deserved their loyalty? The times were too strained to demand anyone's indiscriminate and unwavering adherence. Günter was the best warning. This very day he would try to show Ona a different attitude. Perhaps the girl's enthusiasm was not irresponsible. The capitalist world he had left behind had its ugly face, too— though by now (it had been three years since he'd last visited it) he wasn't sure it wasn't irresistible. Because any world at all, if a man undertakes to improve it, or destroy it for that matter, becomes irresistible. Oh, yes! perhaps Freud was right in speaking of the malaise of culture. The dream the other night, was it a desire for reconciliation and harmony, a gleam of his pure militant's passion of old? Then he thought: What if fear should be dictating all this analysis? What if all this recanting is just the result of a moral and ideological poverty? Well then, I'm no more than a side-show charlatan.

Happy Günter, returning to a nation with all its history vivid before it, with all its horror behind; happy in being a healthy creature of abundance—his political nonconformity was merely the result of too much protein! His adolescent anarchist years would be kneaded into the system. At least he had had practical as well as theoretical experience.

He looked at Luisa as she slept. Here lay his only

possible choice—to adapt, to make love. He didn't want to wake her. He drank his coffee in silence, in slow sips, until he heard steps on the stairs and put down the cup and dressed quickly. It was fear. The steps wrenched away his self-control. The closer they came, the stiffer he grew, from his feet on up to his head. He could not think, he could only listen to those steps getting louder and louder. When they stopped in front of his door, a hoarse voice called him by name. He yanked open the door and it was Günter, his eyes red from his vigil, his lanky hair tangled and tossed, his face weary yet eager. He was wearing the cream-colored sports coat he used on special occasions and the out-of-fashion tie that he had brought with him three years ago, and was carrying a small suitcase.

As soon as he crossed the threshold, he dropped into the armchair in the library, sighing. "Country full of lunatics," he said.

Julio cried out to him to tell him what had happened.

"The sports delegation that went to Puerto Rico was coming back last night and they closed the airport. No planes taking off. Fidel was waiting; I don't think they've arrived yet. The police gave me ten pesos to get back to the hotel and told me to leave the country by myself. At the airport I was told I could probably leave tomorrow night. Can you imagine? I didn't want to take a taxi. I took a bus and came straight to you."

"You can never figure anything out here," Julio said. It was strange how all the tension was gone. Luisa came to the door.

"What do you think of this?"

"Incredible."

"One more day in Cuba," Günter said, with a smile that didn't quite efface the marks his long sleeplessness had left on him.

"You must be dead," Luisa said. "I'll fix you some coffee."

"But you don't have to go back to the hotel," Julio said.

"I think it's the most prudent thing. Everything is so unpredictable. And, Julio, I'd like to see Ara. You might help me."

"Wouldn't it be better to see her here?"

"No, I'd rather do it like the other times, have her come to the hotel. From there we could come back here. And I can get a couple of bottles of rum from a Venezuelan fellow who doesn't even know they've thrown me out. He has dollars. He's offered several times to buy me anything I need. He's a nice guy; I'll ask him to buy me some canned meat. I'm sure he'll do it. I'll tell him it's a gift for Ara. He knows her situation. We can meet here this afternoon."

"All right," Julio said. Luisa came in with two cups of coffee. "Günter wants to get together this afternoon for a farewell party. The best thing is for you to tell Ara."

Luisa said okay.

"Well then, I'll go back to the hotel."

"I can't offer you a ride, you know . . ."

"Are you mad?" Günter cried, getting up. "I'm leaving right now."

They shook hands. After the coffee, Günter looked more cheerful.

"Ciao," he said, and hurried down the stairs.

"Well, I have to be at the hotel early. I still don't

know what I'm going to have to do with the Swedish–
Hungarian–German girl. Hurry up."

"Isn't she nice?" Luisa asked.

"Like all guests—an overflowing amalgam of everything."

But Günter didn't return that night. Nor did it
surprise Julio that he didn't. That was the way his
closest friends and acquaintances had left, overnight. He
never saw Ara again, either. He tried over and over to
get in touch with her, left messages on remote Calle
Luyanó, where she lived, but there was no response. For
Luisa, though, Ara's whereabouts became an obsession.
Four days later, overwrought, exhausted, she finally admitted defeat. She threw herself on the bed and cried.
She could never accept these sudden disappearances,
could never get used to friends and relatives leaving
without a last visit, a "last goodbye," as she said over-
dramatically. What was certain, and she was right in this,
was that every day their isolation became more absolute.
Günter and Ara brought the situation into high relief,
made it more real. Julio hardly dared tell her that Ona,
too, had been cut off from him, unexpectedly.

When he had gone to the hotel two days earlier, she
was no longer waiting for him. Günter was right. They
were on his trail, they were following him, in spite of
his work as an interpreter; probably they had found
someone else to take his place.

"I feel as if I'm being slowly strangled," Luisa said,
sobbing. "I don't know what they intend to do with us."
She looked at him with a desolation that destroyed him.

"To hell with all of them!" he shouted. "They're not
going to sink me."

She stood. "But don't you see that that's just what

they've done? That they've driven us mad, that we're
beating our heads against a stone wall that we can never
break through?"

Defenselessness made her more sensual to him, infused him with a protective emotion mixed with desire.
It was at those times that he could love her most deeply,
could master her whole being. She went toward the
model children's park that was so much a dream and so
much a nightmare. Without glancing up at him, without
uttering another word, she began to caress the diminu-
tive objects in it.

But he couldn't tolerate any more scenes like this.
They nauseated him; love was bright and should always
smell good.

He went out into the street. The yards of the houses
were empty—no students, no workers, not even those
damned shadows Zaida and Fernández Junco. He went
directly to ORO, prepared to discuss his situation with
Raimundo, but he wasn't there. He called Humberto
from a public telephone. Sure that no one could be
listening, he told him about his conversation with
Günter, about the men who were undoubtedly following
him, about the Swedish girl's disappearance, about the
maddening isolation closing in on them. Humberto
remained calm; he asked Julio where he was. Julio
almost shouted that he was at ORO, waiting for
Raimundo, but he'd be damned if he'd wait another day
to straighten out this confusion they had created around
him. Humberto told him the best thing was to go back
home, he'd come see him that evening, they'd discuss
everything. Julio agreed and hung up.

At that hour the area seemed shipwrecked in the
undulating haze. Not even December mitigated the heat.

He recognized Leon's house in front of him, almost in ruins. He remembered his words: "Are you for justice or for truth?"

It was the first question the Hungarian asked every time they got embroiled in one of their political arguments. He would bang his fist on the old leather briefcase, the contents of which no one ever knew. He would say he was a commissioner with his own office in the Gómez block (everyone called it that, because the Gómez building was enormous), and he would exclaim: "Are you for justice or for truth? Answer me, sir!" Since, to all of them, the question was meaningless, they didn't answer it; but Leon insisted (they never knew his real name, either) that the two were "very different things." Justice holds that a black man and a white man are equal, but the truth of every day is another thing. Leon had a big, flushed head, cloudy eyes, no gray hair though he was getting on, and the large hands of a peasant. He was too heavy for his height. His suit was faded, his shirt always had the collar buttoned wrong, and his red tie fell on his chest like a tongue. He wandered around with an herbal that, according to him, the Cubans would soon need—an herbal which included all the edible plants of the island, "because there is not the least doubt that hunger is going to strike this country!" "But the people of Cuba have endured hunger for many years, Leon, and now there is a true revolution and socialist-fraternal institutions to wipe out the old miseries."

Leon almost died of laughter, fell gasping into a chair in La Tertulia bookstore, which a Swiss couple were trying to salvage from wind and tide, the only European touch in the cultural life of Havana. "That's how

Nikita is going to kill you—with hunger! Not me, I won't see that hunger, because I'm clearing out of here before you know it."

The young enthusiasts of those years debated with him, not so much to refute his arguments, which nobody paid any attention to anyway, as to tease him, to get him worked up. "You must be some surviving Nazi, some officer who managed to escape to South America like all the others!" This was the only joke that stopped him cold, silenced him, made him go pale. Many people thought he *was* a Nazi; but that trembling, humane figure could not be a Nazi. For the Cubans, the Nazis were more the images of the American actors who portrayed them in the movies than the flesh-and-blood creatures at whose hands Leon had undoubtedly suffered.

One morning, as he was crossing Calle Línea, Julio saw him talking agitatedly to someone in front of the synagogue at 15th and K. Leon motioned to him to come over. "I'm leaving tomorrow," he said, and added, "Do you know that all these people have been shafted too?" Because nationalization had come for all the businesses on Calle Muralla—Havana's Jewish sector, whose name would have been Wall Street in English—and they were all returning to the paths of exile. "To wander over the face of the earth," said Leon in pompous tones, with a nervous laugh, but his face showed the true impact of what he was saying. This was a different Leon, uncertain, quite another man from the sharp disputant of La Tertulia bookstore. His words were passionate, reverberating. He would go to Miami (they would go), where he would be part of the prosperous group from the Calle Muralla, a feverish gray bastion, almost impregnable, built with iron hands in the passion of creation that made of diaspora a frenzy of life.

Being Cuban, Julio had not the least notion what it meant to be a Jew. In Cuba, every foreigner who did not speak with a French or English accent was simply Galician or Polish. Not even his father, doctor and atheist, who had served more than twenty years ago in the Second World War, had ever spoken of Semites or anti-Semites. He called them Poles too, and they never felt it necessary to explain their old lesson to him. Julio's family lived in Old Havana, and his father's office was in the very heart of Calle Muralla. Julio would often accompany him, especially on calls that his father termed "the strangest in the world"—strange because of the languor and muteness of the girls, whose families wanted to help with vitamins and emulsions. Almost all of them were newly arrived; some hardly spoke Spanish —though they lived in the great houses built during Spanish colonial days. His father would do a careful examination of the patient and announce that it was just nervous tension, a kind of chronic state of shock. In the evening, while Julio's family was having dinner, he would tell his mother the terrible stories. He would bang on the table and shout, "The world is screwed up, completely screwed up! And then try to tell me there's a God!"

Julio stopped a second at the café where Raimundo often met with his group, but there was no one there. He called Luisa; the telephone rang insistently; she must have gone out. Braulio and Cuca weren't home either. He hung up in a fury, gasping, and when he turned discovered two unmistakable types he was sure were following him, but he felt no fear. What precisely had been his crime? Where the hell was this madness headed, which perhaps he, only he, was provoking?

He decided to go to the hotel one more time. What he had feared had indeed happened—he saw Ona talking animatedly with Raimundo. He went toward them instinctively, then realized with surprise that she was speaking an emergent language, learned in three weeks, and the girl's audacity plunged him into deep depression. Browned by the sun, radiant, in a flowered dress which left her shoulders bare, Ona was the living picture of affirmation and credulity. And he, wounded as never before, bleeding like a poor devil, indeed like a spurned lover, turned on his heel and fled.

Outside, the weak drizzle of the fluctuating island winter continued to fall. Huge waves broke on the rocks and hurled over the jetty, covering the hotel gardens with a curtain of mist. The wind struck the awnings at the windows, the park sign swung wildly, wet hinges creaking. It was an unreal landscape, lovely and not at all Cuban.

As he went down the sloping hill at the side of the hotel and made the circle toward the Malecón, spray spattered the windshield. The windshield wipers chirped across the spray, trying to keep the glass clear. Automobiles had their headlights on. The sun was a blurred splotch.

In front of the old monument to the *Maine* he slowed down so his tires wouldn't skid on the muddy water. He turned left, where the waves rose higher, and was tempted to go down Calle Línea to avoid the curtain of spray, but that route was congested with other cars that had also thought it would be better. He decided to go on along the Malecón toward the Quinta Avenida tunnel, which was completely hidden by a screen of water. He drove slowly until he passed by the Hotel Riviera and then speeded up and went across through the tunnel, after which the roads paralleling the Quinta Avenida opened up clear, divided from each other by gardens green all year long.

When he got home, he noticed that the windows of the students' houses were hermetically shut, and in neither Gregorio's nor Zaida and Fernández Junco's house was there any perceptible movement. The garden was one large puddle, the trunk of the Bengal fig even blacker than usual, the branches a dark glowing green. At the library window the heavy vines brushed the glass. Tiny frogs with alert, protruding eyes—intelligent eyes that calculated an intelligent distance—hopped about the garden, and there were vulgar, stubborn swallows, too, shifting around among the gray branches, which barely rose above the flooded grass.

He collected some stones and stood near the front of the car watching the animals intently. They fluttered in concerted motion. (He'd made a mistake, not cutting the grass.) They hopped hither and yon, they mixed with no regard for classes, and why shouldn't they try some sort of violence next? The frog should have devoured the lizard but didn't, and the fucking sparrow, what the hell was it doing?

He threw a stone and the birds and the water jumped and then a circle opened and he aimed at the frogs, so agile they left him openmouthed. He ran out of stones, though the animals multiplied and, what's more, never shut up, except to croak again, all at the same time. The more he dodged the mocking of the frogs, the swallows, and the lizards, the more they hopped and fluttered around. Even the little rain-horses (as he had called the splashes of rain when he was a child) came faster and faster; they were like drops of spittle from a mouth that mocked him, comical and cruel.

He climbed the stairs and, soaked, opened the door. He still heard the croaking of the frogs in his ears.

"Is that you, Julio?"

Luisa was bent over the model of the children's park, putting cardboard trees around a miniature gazebo. She put in the last tree and turned. "You're drenched."

"What are you doing?"

"Why don't you change? I finished what I was doing. Change and come here."

Julio went to the bedroom.

"You have a surprise," she told him.

In a second, he heard a pattering. A little black dog was growling and running in and out around the furniture. Julio was in the middle of dressing and his eyes almost popped out of their sockets. "Where'd you get that dog? Where the hell did you get it?" he shouted. "I don't want a dog. I've told you I don't like dogs."

"But she's only two months old, Julio. She's just a puppy. A cocker spaniel, too. So pretty."

"Where'd you get it?"

Luisa picked it up. The puppy was trembling.

"You get rid of it this afternoon, or I'll throw it out the window." He went back into the bedroom.

"I can't stand people that don't like animals," Luisa said disconsolately as she nuzzled the puppy to her face. In the kitchen she made it a bed out of a blanket and

put it in a corner. She closed the door. When she went
back to the library, Julio was standing before the park
model.

"Would you really throw her out the window?"

"Where'd you get it?"

"I found her as I left the office. She was soaking wet
and starving. You'll see—she'll bring us good luck."

"Bitches don't bring anybody good luck. If it were
a male, maybe, but females are good for nothing but
smearing blood and shit all over the house. And in a
few months you've got a houseful of puppies."

"They can't have puppies until they're a year old."

"They start having puppies as soon as they're born.
I don't want a female dog. What are you going to give
it to eat? I'd like to know that."

"Something always turns up. I call her Claudia."

"You're acting like an old maid."

"She has the eyes of an actress. You haven't really
looked at her. I named her Claudia."

He threw up his hands.

"Tell me we can keep her a while, just a little while,"
she pleaded.

"Tomorrow morning you're getting her out of here."

She took his hand. "All right," she said. "You want
me to explain my project to you?"

She adjusted the model a bit and turned on the light.
"I finished it a little while ago. Isn't it nice?"

She began to point out objects, touching them lightly
with her short fingernails—green zones and sandy zones
where children would play, places designed for day-care
centers, different kinds of games (none of them me-
chanical) to stimulate the kids' imaginations, a little

garden house for lunch and naps, simple comfortable cots, and a brake of trees that would provide the natural breezy shade Cuba's climate demanded. The system had been successfully adopted in Finland and Sweden, in spite of their climates. She extolled the economic virtues of the plan. Thousands could be built for a cost insignificant in comparison with the usual day-care centers, which cost thousands of dollars and were counterproductive to the psychological formation of children.

Julio stroked her hair. "I'm glad you dream at least."

"But it's not a dream, Julio," she protested. "A woman, a friend of mine, is ready to bring up the project for debate at the Women's Federation. She's very enthusiastic, and she has a lot of experience in psychology."

"And what good is that?"

"I'm sure they'll listen to her."

"Good luck!" he said disparagingly.

"She can talk to Fidel and explain the project to him personally. If we can do this, everything will change."

"What do you mean, 'everything will change'?"

"I would feel more useful."

"Don't you feel useful doing what you do?"

"I'd feel better if I could see one of my projects become reality one day. You'd feel the same way, you can't deny that."

"Architecture doesn't interest me. It's boring to me."

"Yes—what's interesting to you is politics. In this country it's the only thing that interests anybody. It's what's drowning us. You can be the best architect in your group, but if you care more about a Doric column than about a leader's speech, you'll never get ahead."

"Do you really care so much about getting ahead?"

"Yes, I do," she said, emphatically.

"You want to be more successful than I am, don't you?"

She began to laugh.

He sat back in the chaise longue and she came over to sit beside him. "Sometimes I think you love me."

"Sometimes I do."

"Other times you hate me."

"Very much."

She put her lips to his ear. "You hate me, you'd like to annihilate me. Know why?"

"Tell me."

"Because you're crazy," she whispered.

He gave her a shove that sent her sprawling. "Don't say that even as a joke," he shouted, standing up. "Not even as a joke, do you hear me?! Not even as a joke, goddamnit, not even as a joke!"

"All right, comrade. It shall be as you command," she whispered in an almost strangled voice. "Not even as a joke," she imitated him sarcastically.

"I feel bad—irritated, anxious. One day my head is just going to explode."

"But what's happened to you? Did you have an argument with somebody?"

He said nothing. It would have been futile to speak once again of the toll this persecution was taking on them; but Luisa's state of alarm triggered in him a new anxiety. She didn't look at him as she had other times, but followed his every movement, every reaction of his debility, as though she sensed that it would all end in disaster.

"Don't talk if you don't want to," she said. "But I'll figure out what it is that's really happening to you."

That night he could hardly sleep; he was prey to

troubled dreams, and every time he turned over, he discovered Luisa's open eyes, heard her breathing uneasily at his side. Although he pretended not to see her, he knew those yearning eyes were observing him.

They barely exchanged a word in the morning. She gave him a cup of coffee, which he drank in silence, and then went to get dressed.

"Are you taking me to work?" she asked him cautiously, and he stood up without a word, but she knew she could follow him. Before he dropped her off at the Ministry, she asked him in a low voice to come pick her up, and Julio nodded in silence.

He made the trip back completely absorbed in his thoughts, driving the car mechanically. At the intersection of 23rd and P, he stopped at a red light. When he turned to look in the direction of the Ministry of Labor, he thought he saw someone he knew. A girl dressed in casual, practical working clothes. When the light changed, he had barely gone a few yards when the girl waved in his direction. It was Ona. He opened the passenger door and invited her to get in. The tanned, radiant face looked at him happily.

"I think we've been playing at being corpses," she said. "We've each been living in our own tomb."

"I've been where I always am," Julio said. "And as for you, tombs don't let you get such a nice tan."

Ona broke out laughing. She said to him in Spanish, "Of course, it's the light of Cuba. I'm happy!" And she looked fixedly at him to gauge the effect her words in Spanish produced on him.

"Where can I take you?"

"As in Ibsen, you need only add: 'devil's coachman.'"

Julio suddenly saw as if for the first time that golden head, the short, youthful hair, the young tanned face the color of her hair, golden. He couldn't hold back and said, "You're very pretty today, Ona."

She thanked him, smiling.

"But seriously, are you going to the hotel?"

She hesitated a second before replying. He insisted, "I can take you anywhere you want to go, really."

Slowly, she said, "I'll take you at your word. Take me anywhere."

All said and done, these sudden insinuations of the woman were superior to the macho's grotesque beating around the bush. Ona hadn't needed very many words to take him where she wanted. Sociologist or not, she now counted him among the collection of casual, random samples that her interest had gathered. But he liked the way she was, her hair, her eyes, her skin, the freedom and naturalness with which she filled the worker's outfit she had just bought. He was impressed by the decisiveness with which she came naked to him, with which she embraced him, took off his shirt, and pressed her mouth to his skin. He held her at arm's length for a second, looking at her lips before kissing her over and over again. He was no longer conscious of what he did; he surrendered, without thinking. All his intelligence was reduced to the fiery possession of that body, and he sank into her with a mixture of tenderness and hatred. Under him, those eyes looked at him with such an intensity that Julio felt a sudden chill. They were distant, impersonal eyes, almost critical, firmly fixed on him.

"What's wrong?"

[1 4 5]

"Nothing," she groaned, but he heard her crying. It was a controlled weeping, selfish, like the weeping that Luisa couldn't share with him—a painful emotion that didn't include him, was foreign to him.

"What's wrong?"

"Nothing, nothing, really. Go on." And she squeezed him tightly, but he began to sweat; blood stopped flowing to his sex.

"I can't."

He stood up quickly and got dressed. He fled the room, where Ona went on crying.

The naked body, the beautiful girl's body would not fade from his memory. Though Luisa wept as she did, though the image of his woman—especially in the crisis of helplessness which she often brought to sex—interfered, the body of Ona stayed.

He remembered that Luisa had asked him to pick her up at the Ministry and he went to get her. He went several times around the parking lot, but he didn't see her. Then he left the car where he usually left it and went into the café to call her.

He asked her to come down and go straight to the car.

On his way out, he ran into Braulio.

"Hi, Julio," he said, putting a hand on his shoulder, smiling. His alert eyes, noble and somehow sly, accompanied a heavy twisted nose. His beard was salted with gray, but his hair was as it had been fifteen years ago. He asked Julio if he was going to Miramar.

"No. Today is Friday. First I have to go by El Vedado," Julio said with a smile of shared understanding. "You know that. If you want, I can drop you off there."

"Thanks, Julio. The buses are hellish, especially at this time of day. What about Luisa?"

"In the car."

"And how's your work?"

"Okay."

"Raimundo is happy. He says your translations are impeccable. And González likes them, too. Everybody is very pleased, and that's good, Julio."

When he talked, he always looked for happy circumstances, and he smiled with the skill of a man who has laboriously practiced enthusiasm. In everything, he always sought out the agreeable angle, a rosy tint, a good omen even in bad appearances. He practiced a love for justice that did not exclude either the believer or the atheist, and his favorite word was "love." Many times this word had, justly, saved him. Julio had a great affection for him; he liked his way of being delighted to have survived, which made him an exemplary man and a child, and liked, too, those sly sweet eyes that Julio thought he could read. They walked toward the parking lot, and Julio told Braulio his dream about Fidel Castro. Braulio listened, fascinated, as Julio drew out every nuance of the conversation, and, of course, the cordial tone of it in the dream. Braulio kept saying "Of course," as though he had known it all beforehand.

"What do you think?"

"What do you mean, what do I think? It's a sign." Braulio lowered his voice, and Julio laughed. Braulio stopped a few steps from the parking lot. He squeezed Julio's arm and whispered through his beard: "He's going to call you."

"Who?"

"Who do you think, dummy?"

"Are you crazy? He doesn't even know who I am."

"That's what you think. He knows a hell of a lot more than you think."

"But, Braulio, you're talking exactly like a character out of the dream."

"Listen, Julio, listen, it gives me goosebumps." He slid three fingers of his right hand over his left arm. "It gives me goosebumps, because you don't know anything about these things. And it can't be explained by Marxism. It's a sign. Because, look, how would you explain that dream?"

"There are lots of ways."

"Circumlocutions. That's all. But explaining it, I mean the definition of the word 'explain,' nobody can do that."

Julio laughed again.

"Well, you leave me to my spirits. What's more, I think about you all the time. Cuca and I pray for you. If I could have a consultation with you, I'd do it this very afternoon. But I don't want to, it's not the place." Then he paused and asked with unexpected gravity, "Would you do it?" He shook his head. "No, you'd laugh."

"Would I *what*?"

"You're too cutting, superficial, cold. You'd insult me."

"Tell me. I swear to you I wouldn't do anything like that."

[1 4 8]

"Would you come with me, Julio? You say when. You know my sister-in-law and she likes you. She's an extraordinary medium. Listen to me, Julio."

"Well, why not? One of these days. Call me."

Braulio was transformed. He put a hand on Julio's shoulder and walked toward the car.

"How's my love?" he said, kissing Luisa on the cheek.

"Don't speak to me. You haven't been to see us in three weeks. It would take a miracle," said Luisa.

"But that office doesn't leave me a minute to drop you a line, let alone pay a visit. Everything is translation and work. And when I get home, between Cuca, the girls, and the market, there's not a second left over. But this weekend, absolutely, we'll get together."

"I told Braulio the dream," said Julio, getting in behind the wheel.

"Oh? What did he say?"

Braulio got in next to Luisa. Julio started the engine.

"It still gives me goosebumps," Braulio said, and rubbed his fingers over his arm again.

They went along Calle Aguiar, headed for Empedrado, so they could go straight up to Avenida del Puerto, to get out of the narrow streets of Old Havana as quickly as possible. The blinding light of midday at the end of December blazed on the silver cupola of the National Observatory and over the brilliant oil-slicked asphalt.

"The heat is terrible," said Braulio.

"And Julio says the weather has changed," said Luisa, winking conspiratorially at Braulio.

"Well, I'll bet anything that tonight is the first cool night of the year," said Julio.

"Our little autumn in the suburbs," added Braulio.

When they got on the Malecón, a pleasant breeze filled the automobile; but when they went up Calle 23, in the direction of El Vedado, it became oppressive again.

"Are you sure you couldn't read anything of what he wrote on the paper?" Braulio asked.

"I already told you no."

"Maybe you've forgotten," said Luisa.

"I've forgotten whole parts of my dreams and the curious thing is that days later I've dreamed the same thing over again," said Braulio.

"There are recurrent dreams. I dream very little."

"You dream awake," Luisa stated.

"A lot of the fantasy that we pour out during the day is a form of dreaming," interjected Julio.

"Hasn't it ever happened to you two that you're looking at something, anything, and it begins to fall to pieces?" Luisa asked.

"It happens to me all the time," Julio asserted.

"Sometimes when I'm eating, I can look at a table and imagine what would happen if I were to rip off the tablecloth right under the noses of the people sitting there," Luisa went on.

"Quite a commotion, probably," said Braulio, smiling.

"I who argue with books am even worse."

Braulio hooted with laughter. "When I shave, I talk to myself and hit the girls over the head with shoes every time they start yelling. I see blood running down their heads and then see the hospital and me explaining all this and holding and kissing the girls, feeling terribly guilty."

When they came to 26th, Julio turned left and went toward the Acapulco movie house.

"See that line of aluminum posts?" he asked.

"Yes," Luisa said.

"What about them?" asked Braulio.

"I was thinking that one movement of my hand would be enough to smash us to a pulp." And he laughed.

"Julio!" Luisa exclaimed.

"Don't joke about such things, Julio," Braulio said, earnestly.

"One movement, you know? Almost imperceptible. Just one and everything goes to shit, Braulio, to the world of your spirits."

The rest of the trip they were silent. In front of the movie, Julio braked smoothly.

"You're getting diabolical," said Braulio.

"Why?" Julio asked, with a smile.

"Yes, a devil," Luisa agreed.

"And even though you're kidding, I'll be thinking about you, I'll be praying for you," said Braulio as he left the car. He kissed Luisa on the cheek.

"Will we see each other this weekend?" Luisa said.

"Yes." Braulio tried to hide his uneasiness.

" 'Bye," called Julio, and stomped the accelerator.

In the rearview mirror he saw Braulio waving. When he put the car into third, he brought it to its normal speed.

"Do I make you nervous?"

"You're cruel, you're nasty to your friends, even the ones who love you most."

Julio squeezed her thigh without looking at her. In a while he said, "You know what I'm thinking?"

"No."

"What I'd like to do now?"

"No."

"Go in over there"—he pointed out a yellow building surrounded by trees and a wall—"and pull your clothes off in front of a mirror and beat you to a pulp, pulverize you—and then make love to you very tenderly."

Luisa's eyes filled with tears. "Is that what you'd really like?" She spoke in a strangled voice.

Julio stopped at the corner of the park on 26th, in front of one of the billboards with Eduardo's face on it. "Yes, that's what I'd like," he said, pursing his lips.

"Then you're a sadist. Do you know that's what you are?"

"Maybe."

"But sadists don't love."

"Yes, they do."

"Sadists don't love anyone," she insisted. "No one."

Julio started the car and headed toward Miramar.

"Every day is worse. Isn't that so?"

"Yes," she said quietly. "I thought so many years would be enough."

"But you were wrong."

"Yes. But you can't help it, because you're just like all Cubans."

"Yes, we're all alike," he said.

"Capable of living your whole life in love with some English whore, but incapable of admitting one percent of that experience to a Cuban woman. You'd never marry a woman like that."

"Marvelously put," he said. "That's what I think."

"You'll never marry me, I know that," Luisa said with a strange serenity.

"I'll never marry you and you know it," he repeated. "Exactly like the other men you've known. I don't see why I should break the precedent."

"Yes. That's machismo."

"Machismo," he repeated sarcastically.

"We could have ten revolutions in this country and the situation of women would still be the same. It's the only point on which revolutionaries and counterrevolutionaries agree."

"Oh, sure," he said ironically, "because revolutions, I don't know if you're aware of it, as a general rule are made by males. It's not at all surprising that they apply their own rules and principles."

"You call anything principle."

"Well, nastiness or prejudice or whatever," he said. "The male is the male and he's the one who imposes the conditions. You can accept them or reject them. For example, I don't force you to be with me. You're with me because you want to be. If a woman, you for instance, had enough dignity, she wouldn't accept those conditions. She would rebel against them. Why don't they? A man, however imbecilic he might be, would never accept a woman's conditions. Why doesn't the same thing ever happen with women?"

"You're so primitive, Julio. You can spend whole hours discussing politics and theoretical books and philosophers and even you aren't capable of answering those questions."

"Of course I am. You're the one who can't answer them. You've never been able to. Your own ideas are changeable and accommodating. Before you started living with me, you didn't ask for freedom for women. On the contrary. You just wanted to settle down with a man —maybe have a family—and when we started living together, you suddenly began spouting the same morals as every woman who ever spread her legs."

"You talk like the most primitive man on earth."

"I am, sweetheart," he cried. "I am, and I like being that way, and I can't be any other way, hear me?"

"I know," she said. "Even if you wanted to be, you couldn't be any other way." And she began to cry.

When they got home, they went upstairs without saying a word. Julio turned on the air conditioner and took off his tie. He could hear water from the taps and Luisa rinsing her face, as she did when she cried. He heard her open the bathroom door and come into the bedroom.

"The only thing you know how to do is cry."

"Leave me alone."

She sat down at the dressing table and began to brush her hair. He fell on the bed, looking at her from the back. Then she turned around on the seat, completely naked; tears streamed down onto her cool thighs, and when he went to sit up, an enormous pressure dropped on his shoulders, pinning him immobile. He wanted to scream and felt a gag go over his mouth and an infinitely fine cord cut into his feet and hands. Sure that he could not get up, Luisa made an arrogant gesture with her hand. Her eyes were brilliant, her mouth was half open, and she fell on the chaise longue, under the weight of a young man who moved over her thighs and belly with a desperate and expert rhythm. Was that Eduardo's face?

"What are you thinking about?"

"Nothing," he said coldly.

"I know," she said. "I know exactly what you're thinking."

"Tell me then."

"Evil people all think the same thing."

[1 5 4]

"Tell me what."

"You're thinking of how to put a chastity belt on me."

"No," he said, "that wasn't what I was thinking."

For he went on thinking about Ona, and not even when Luisa came and turned off the light, pressing herself against him—something they always did, in spite of the fiercest arguments—did he stop thinking about Ona, though now he felt the blood flow again to his sex.

"Stop that," said Luisa. "You can't want to make love at this hour."

"No," he said.

"That's what you always say. I know you perfectly."

His exhaustion dragged him down into a long sleep; he knew it because the violent slap that knocked him out of it didn't make him sour as he usually was when Luisa told him to wake up, it was late. He lazily, pleasantly opened his eyes; he paid no attention when he saw her a few steps from the bed, dressed in the little tailored suit she had worn for three straight winters, carrying the small suitcase that easily held the few things she possessed. He touched his face where Luisa had hit him, and felt puzzled, confused.

Luisa looked at him with fury. "That's the last straw!" she screamed.

"What the hell are you talking about? Are you crazy?"

"Look in the mirror."

He lay back on the bed. She grabbed him by the hair and made him look at the large dresser mirror, showing him the tooth marks on his right shoulder.

"You've been telling me all this time that they've separated you and that Swedish whore and now it seems the little Swedish thing has almost chewed your shoulder off. Accusing the government of persecuting you, of following your every step, yours and all your resentful little friends', who're all no more than a bunch of shameless pimps, like that Günter, who never did anything but exploit that poor black Ara. I'm sick of your resentments, of the life you've made me live. You accuse Fidel Castro of being ambitious, but nobody is more ambitious than you are. You'd like to put a zipper on my vagina, so you could go on sleeping with anybody you wanted to, while you reproach me all the time about my life with poor Eduardo, while you go on looking at the billboards like you're crazy. But listen, *I'm* not crazy! You're a shit macho, a big puritanical Catholic shit, adoring the Virgin Mary because she conceived by the grace of the Holy Spirit! It horrifies you that a simple, mere male could have had anything to do with making the son of God! I'm tired of your whole dirty mind, all the time you've spent talking to me about purity. For you the ideal woman was Beatrice, Beatrice, Beatrice! Your childhood sweetheart! But to this day I haven't seen a photograph, a letter, one single piece of evidence that she existed. All of you machos should have your necks wrung, like Fidel Castro says. Well, keep your Swedish piece, your Beatrice, because I'm leaving."

Unable to react, half naked, immobile in the bed, he saw her open and close the door and heard her going down the stairs.

He put on his pants and shirt and shoes as quickly as he could and ran to the window. At that moment Luisa was getting on a number 32 bus, which disappeared among the trees of the Quinta Avenida. Julio took himself to the kitchen and, as he always did in moments of anxiety, drank a glass of water, but it didn't produce the slightest coolness in his dry mouth. He took several slow, disoriented steps and stopped in the shadows at the entrance to the hallway, where the seven bedrooms had been closed off for three years. He pressed the switch and a light at the end of the hallway went on. The rest of the hall was still dark. The fluorescent tubes gave off a stain of light only at their ends, since the transformers were so old. In a corner he saw his mother's big solid trunk of black leather with the four metal bands strapped around it like belts.

When he was a child, he had hidden in it. His mother and aunts would search desperately for him when it was time to leave, when he would refuse to take the train which every two or three years, depending on the ups and downs of the family's financial situation, would take them to his grandparents' farm. Panting in the trunk, he would spy on the movements of his aunts, who, dressed in black, with their big hats and great handbags, would be closing the doors and windows of the house he didn't want to leave.

"I knew you were going to come."

He couldn't determine for a moment where the voice came from, but it was unmistakably his mother's.

"And what's more, you deserved it."

The legs, extraordinarily thin, impatiently moved over the trunk, over the old schooner of his childhood.

"Mother, tell me what she says isn't true. You knew Beatrice."

"Baloney." His mother dismissed the whole question with an exaggerated gesture.

"We played together when we were children, Ma. You'd sit on the dock to watch us play."

"Baloney. You're obsessed by Beatrice and this hoyden. What nonsense they make you go through! You should have gotten out of this country; but you've always been a renegade, just like your father and grand-father. The only thing you're good for is to make us suffer."

She stood straight and stomped around recklessly, almost burying her heels in the leather top of the trunk, still prey to her old habits as a teacher, for she walked on the trunk as though she were still on the little dais at school, with her eyes raised, the pointer in her hand, and her fleshy lips forming, syllable by syllable, each question. That voice, that imperiousness, that self-assurance and commanding attitude which startled the

daydreamers, were his mother. The whole class trembled, but not him.

"Easy. Throw dirt on us. You and the hoyden in three
rooms, and the rest dark. How many times have you
come to see your mother's picture? Answer me, how
many?"

They would call him, they would look for him beginning early in the morning. Caruca helped carry down
the bedroom furniture, while Lucrecia exerted herself
in pulling out lamp cords. They called to him and called
to him, but without any real urgency. He knew those
sharp little cries they had kept his father's and grandfather's wakes with, the stamp of their tribulations and
senile sourness.

Caruca, skinny, taciturn, wrapped in the clothes in
which she had sweated through all the family mourn-
ings, full of aberration and pomposity, wet now with
perspiration, still had the spirit to help load the last
piece of furniture into the truck; Lucrecia gathered up
the religious prints, leaving a row of white spaces along
the walls. From the trunk, peering through a crack in
the lock, Julio would watch the house little by little
being emptied. His dog Tin cowered in a corner, with-
drawn and alien. They would go on calling "Julio,
Julio, Julio" and would go into his mother's bedroom.
"Come out, Julio, once and for all . . ." They would
push open the door: "Come out, now." But they
couldn't find him. They picked up pieces of furniture
as though they were bundles of laundry. The legs of the
china cabinet dragged on the kitchen floor (but Caruca
didn't flinch); they seemed the great black masts of a
ghost ship. His mother crossed the driveway and went

straight to the truck, helping to load the chest as though depositing her last hope, and called and looked in the pantry, under beds, in the attic, among the accumulations of three generations which had lived in that house with an almost ritual constancy, but his was a name called to the wind, to no one. Even his dog took off, running.

"Under the bed," Caruca would say. "He's bound to be under the bed. He always does that; we'll pull him out later." And they went on, attending to the furniture, trying to erase the traces of a long stay in a house that had withheld happiness from them. The house was surrounded by a laurel grove.

The neighbors, since early in the morning, had followed the unwonted bustle. There had been little groups behind Venetian blinds since the moving van had stopped in front of the house and his aunts had begun to load furniture into it as though that were the most natural thing in the world. Now, later, skinny, shriveled up, making her way through the high grass of the arbor, Caruca was even uglier and more unkempt than in the morning. Lucrecia said something to her about a train, but she kept looking, separating the high grass with her hands, scrabbling right down to the last little stones. She had started calling again and tapping on her high heels, and he could predict with precision the second phase of her hysterical cries. Lucrecia was holding Tin in her arms (Tin, trying to free himself from that skinny grasp); she said something about the train again. But Caruca went on chirping, her eyes brilliant, her face sweaty. On her back a swath of sweat widened and a patch, too, under her arms. Dirt covered her shoes, burrs stuck to her clothes, though she tried, vainly, to brush them off.

The blinds in the neighboring houses moved shamelessly, the heads waggled brazenly, watching them. But his aunts, oblivious, kept shrieking and running in circles. Tin went on trying to free himself from the skinny grasp of Lucrecia, and Juan Valdés, the truck driver, went on throwing ropes over the furniture, ignoring the shouting, tying the ends, and Lucrecia and Caruca kept on closing the windows and doors of the empty house, and they were already hoarse. They burped disgustingly, Caruca wrapped in her black shawl. Lucrecia sat down on the steps of the porch that opened onto the arbor and pretended to cry (and Julio knew her last resort was to try to make him come out that way, by making him feel bad). And his name resounded as though in a cave: " 'Ulio! 'Ulio! 'Ulio!" Caruca came along then and dropped down onto the broken wooden step. She had locked all the doors; the key was in her dirty fingers, and Tin wrenched to get free of the skinny claw. The grove was filling with shadow, and a little wind began to blow, almost like autumn, but there were very few leaves on the ground. Lucrecia said something about the train, it was an imperceptible whisper, and Tin growled and trembled.

Then Julio raised the lid of the trunk a crack, savored the triumph of those hours, undefeated in his hiding place, as he heard them scold and cry. He walked barefoot through the darkened house, through the bedrooms. In his own, he looked at the empty spaces, the white stains where the photographs had been that somehow summed up his life. He went to the window and, sure

[1 6 1]

that his aunts would never find him, jumped out into the garden, went to the arbor and silently, trembling in the chill of the evening, observed the house. It was alone now, abandoned, in the midst of its grove of laurel trees, almost inches from the river, white, with red tiles, and a dormer window above—what house is not beautiful? All paths finally led there, all the dogs in the neighborhood came to play with Tin, and Tin was friendly and happy and his aunts had to keep him indoors, though Lucrecia would have been delighted to "fix" him—she had an old maid's special spite for him. Her sleep was frighteningly light, and she seemed to follow him through his night wanderings. In the morning, in the kitchen, while she waited for the milk to boil on the stove, she would stare fixedly between Tin's legs as though she wanted to crush his balls.

That time of the evening was when punctually one heard the sound of the motor that seemed to encircle the house. His grandfather and his mother came down and joined the aunts. His mother asked where he was. He could picture her every reaction, the degrees of her anxiety, even her restlessness. Only she had the instinct, almost animal, to find him. She came toward the grove, emitted the unique, unchanging call that extended through time, reproachful and authoritarian: "Julio, are you there? Are you there?" The third time she called, she disarmed him. He answered, faltering, vanquished: "Yes, Mama, I'm here." Later that evening, on the train, a kind of reconciliation took place. Everyone sat down together, and when they spoke to him, it was in tired, protective tones.

. . .

"Why don't you answer me? How many times? You don't dare say none, you who covered us with dirt, me and the aunts—you and your hoyden in three rooms, and the rest of them dark."

She went on pacing back and forth on the trunk, but her face at that angle had a yellow, aged look. He wondered how old his mother would be now. How long ago had he stopped celebrating her birthdays with her? Lucrecia and Caruca would start early in the morning gathering candles, kneading the flour, the bread, the eggs, whipping the egg whites. An enormous cake, mouths whose breath became weaker every year, a circle of thin hands with pulses that echoed and filled his ears, a single, long kiss and a little saliva on his face.

"Can't you hear me, Julio? Are you there? Answer me. Are you there?"

"Yes, Mama, I'm here. I've been here for thirty-five years."

They lifted him up, they dandled him, they kissed him, they passed him from arm to arm. The odors from the ovens left a lingering taste on his palate. He heard guitars behind the houses, the choruses of country people under the trees, then the pig's squealing, but his mother cheated him of that vision of the end. For him there was the moment afterwards when the skin turned golden in the fire and the smell of oregano and guava leaves impregnated the air. They went from house to house, he and his mother. There was no uncle or cousin that he did not visit with her. She was robust and lively and had great black alert eyes and fleshy lips; she spoke with impressive self-confidence.

[1 6 3]

"Want to see God?" His Uncle Anselmo, a plump canary six feet tall, covered Julio's ears with the palms of his rough hands and raised him to the height of his forehead and turned him loose then, leaving him with a droning buzz in his ears and a burning in his temples which took hours to go away.

"Leave him alone." His mother took him in her arms and kissed him, and "He's a brute," she said, scolding the uncle—warm and protective against his waves of laughter.

The dust cloud of December, the droughts, the great plantings of tobacco which reached almost to the height of the gates made of rounded tiles, and he and his mother, here and there, always walking.

"You want to run? Let's go, I'll catch you in the aralias."

He would run toward the pillars of green trees which surrounded the house and would hide behind the tallest one, in the thick, abundant leaves, and he would see her coming toward him with great strides.

"Where has that boy got to?" She pretended not to find him. "Julio!" He circled the tree trunk, staying out of sight. "Where can he have gotten to?" And she would look all around, except the place where he had hidden. "Are you there, Julio? Answer me. Are you there?"

And he would stick his head out between the plants, smiling, running toward her. "Yes, Mama, I'm here."

And she would lift him up and with him in her arms would walk the last stretch of the path to home.

"Button your shirt. I don't like to see you with your shirt open. And it's all yellowed. Women today don't even know how to wash clothes. And the house smells like shit, they've stuck you with a dog in the house. You're skinny and jumpy as a cat, you look like a chinchilla. I didn't raise you to live like this. I bet you've even forgotten how to swim."

She turned, her legs spread like a tuning fork, planting her heels on the very ends of the trunk, showing off. "Look at me—old, tough, and light on my feet."

He had never liked to see her jump around like that —much less now.

"See?" She spoke to him from the chandelier, teetering, he couldn't watch, as masterful as a trapeze artist. With a single motion she was hanging from the fixture, her bent knees draped over the brass support. Her thin, wrinkled thighs were naked, and he saw the shadow of her pelvis and the shining lace and felt the sudden chill, the horror, of seeing her leap from the chandelier into the laurel grove, with a wet greasy plumage, like the owl in the picture books, reciting in a warble the never-ending story of what's your name, puddin' and tain, ask me again and I'll tell you the same, what's your name, puddin' and tain, ask me again and I'll . . .

He hardly dared call her by name (he always did, in her old age, when he wanted to scold her—the child aged and the parent behaving like a child), and he could barely manage to say to her, shout at her, "Ana," since she was all a mass of leaves and feathers.

Another problem was that he stumbled on the dust-covered, abandoned trunk. He opened it and sifted, tremulous, through the old photographs, some ribbons, diplomas, letters (the first he received from his aunts). He closed the lid and went out into the hall, feeling his way along the walls so as not to stumble. When he came to the fire-escape door, he felt the blow of the latch on his forehead and a burning on his breast. He tried to open the door, but the rusted latch would not give; he persisted, the hinges creaked, and he managed to turn the doorknob until the door opened. Leaves were scattered all over the circular metal staircase. It was getting late; there were signs of a storm in the sky. The humid air relieved him, cooled him. He descended slowly, shoving aside the dirt and leaves with his shoes. A drizzle, almost a mist, hung over the garden.

"Ana, please come in. You're going to get a chill." He came down the last step, moving aside the leaves of the vine that almost completely covered the handrail and the rusty seats. "You're going to catch cold, Ana. Come in, I'll explain it to you."

He heard laughter behind him, from the top of the chipped wall. A group of bricklayers were watching him with a grin. Two were whitewashing the gate of the students' house, another was stirring lime in a huge vat, and the oldest of them came up carrying a pail of water, which he poured over the thick white mixture.

"Hello," stammered Julio timidly. "Lots of work?"

The one stirring the lime answered, smiling but not looking at him. "Well, yes; building socialism here."

Julio essayed a smile, trying to come up with some cheerful expression of solidarity. "And communism, comrade. Fidel said that both will be built at the same time."

The bricklayer looked at him for the first time. "Hear that, Pedro? He says both are going to be built together, so pour another bucket of shit in here."

And the group broke into a howl of laughter. What was taking her so long? She was getting soaked in the rain. Why wouldn't she come in? Why did she keep him

there, vulnerable, exposed to the mockery of that scum?
Wasn't he getting soaked too, standing there in his
muddy shoes? And this fucking freezing nylon shirt.
Shit country, summer all year, goddamn, and the fucking cold when you least expect it. The pines he hadn't
trimmed drenched him completely, and the old woman
over there on the mount of laurels. How tall is this tree?
Too big. There was no one anymore to bother about the
garden. Where had all the gardeners gone? Old man
Fernández Junco swore they were all in the National
Institute of Tourism, but Zaida said they were in the
army, that the youngest had been sent to Russia. You
have to keep a garden pruned back, goddamnit, cut it,
cut it, cut it.

"How much will you charge me?"
"Wait a minute, hold on."
The gardener had measured the long plot with his
eyes, and Luisa said she'd especially like the begonias
taken care of. She was self-possessed and open that day.
The gardener looked at her slyly, but it didn't go un-
noticed by Julio. Well, let the grass swallow them up.
He was glad when the gardener answered Luisa's
question.
"Money? What do I want it for? Clothes, if you have
any, okay, and shoes—*things*. You can't eat money,
miss."
A month later, Julio saw him prowling around in the
garden. He liked the hoyden, the old goat. He went out
and found the man in a corner—dressed weirdly, in
clothes and shoes that must have come from abroad.
"Don't you remember me?"

"Yes," said Julio.

"The grass keeps growing. It's going to swallow up the house."

"And us with it," said Julio. "There's nobody anymore who wants to do this kind of work. I was hoping I'd find somebody."

"Look, my friend, you're not going to find anybody. Take my word for it. People steer clear of this kind of work. I don't want money; I want things. Listen, for example, right now I'm working with foreigners. Diplomats get along well with me. Do you like whiskey? If you want some, you know, a hundred bucks."

"What are you talking about?"

"Get off it, you can trust me. Italian shoes, too, and nylon socks, colored socks."

"I don't need anything." Julio got into the car and started the motor.

The sallow face persisted against the car window. "I can come back, huh? Anytime you say."

He jerked away when Julio backed up the car and turned toward the Quinta Avenida.

The grass almost reached up to the ficus trees at the fence and, against the grillwork, made a green compact wall. From his bedroom, it looked like a symmetrical wood, but now he saw that the hibiscus and the night-blooming jasmine stretched to the height of the window. There were birds' nests, and lizards jumped from branch to branch, and thorny bougainvillea scratched at his shirt and face. There were no gardeners and there never would be gardeners again. The house would become a ruin among the weeds; wild lianas would cover it; no amount of volunteer work could return it to its original state. He had always believed that things live and men vegetate, that the very inertia and impassivity of things established a degree of resistance against erosion, against time; but now he saw that those dirty wet walls were also part of the dark, active trembling of people, that that crack widening behind the thick sinews of the vine was a kind of death, a wound. Time weighed on things, too; everything in life shared gravity and ruin.

The fine drizzle of a while ago, almost a mist, became heavier. Wet stones scattered along the paths glistened; there were puddles everywhere; and when he tried to get to the fence, he slipped and almost fell. The wind made swirls in the distance; the Quinta Avenida was flooding, and the fallen leaves piled up on the sewer gratings in a turbid, agitated ring of water. He knew those sudden storms of the tropics, the squall that could last minutes or a rainstorm which lasted for days and which in a rough way marked the limits of the seasons. He figured—his whole being went into the calculation —that this was the beginning of one of those days-long stretches of bad weather, and he was terrified at the thought that this nourishing water would make the grass even taller and that leaks no one could repair would further weaken the ceiling. He turned and went toward an opening in the undergrowth, an esplanade where the vegetation became shorter and more accessible, less intricate. He looked through the grillwork, where branches left a small circle like a ship's porthole, and he saw, or thought he saw, that the very trees were bending on the Quinta Avenida, in a confused firmament, a flat sheet of wind and water—a turbid sky with no birds, a neuter ghostly frame against which three gray swaying trees stood out like blades of a fan or a windmill.

"Ana, come on, why won't you just come in? Why do you want to make yourself sick, or make me sick?"

An indistinct shape stirred among the branches, long and thick, like a goat's leg, frightened wet eyes and short dripping ears.

"Ana," he groaned, trying to hold back the emptiness, but his shoe slipped on the muddy ground and he fell full-length on his back, with a pain in the nape of his neck, his arms and legs spread-eagled, the rain pouring down on his face, blinding him. The dog jumped over branches and ran off, growling.

"Malum signum," he stammered.

The water seeped into his ears, his shoulders sank into the puddle's cold, oppressive current, and he floated among tree roots and fallen flowers; his eyelids were heavy. They closed and his only landscape was what he saw through a red film of blood and poison, like a man sick with fever. A mob of soldiers were cutting through the vines, opening a way through the interminable woods, and every severed branch throbbed in his temples as though it were a living part of his organism. He managed to pull himself together and stand up, feeling light and renewed in the reddening afternoon; a single word of his, rapid and imperative, could wipe them all out. And he began to run through the garden, making strange, efficient circles, as though he moved through the very heart of magic. With a loose stick from the vine arbor, he confronted the advancing columns. Behind the rusty visors, he divined eyes of horror. He swung the shield about and brandished the shining lance before which they could do nothing but retreat.

And he leaped like a young Palestinian guerrilla over
arches of flame, in those exhausting training exercises,
and he struck out all around, making the iron shields
clang. They were all heroes, heroes of all sizes and ages
—heroes suddenly as puzzled as clumsy, frightened
children, heroes who moved like lancers to the sound
of fife and flute, heroes from remotest history and from
today, moving like leeches but so downhearted and
inept—straw men (as though *he* needed practice!) to
show off his skill. At an imperious sign of his shield they
knelt—thousands of rusted heads and backs, a yellowish
ramp like a path of paving tiles; at another signal they
bent their heads to the ground and opened their iron
jaws. They grazed—on all fours they cut the greenery
with their teeth. They devoured branches, tree trunks,
flowers, they fed on that hateful shade, they sank deeper
and deeper into the mud and entered the glistening
humus of this solar earth. And as they sank they
brandished their useless weapons, which would never
again destroy. Children would come later, or a council
of old men, under the clean vines returned to their
original innocence, purged of history. He wanted this
deluge to swallow everything—acts, speeches and
apothegms, philosophers and enchanters, prophets and
kings and secretaries-general and bishops of all churches.

A man alone, a lance, a shield alone in a dense shelter-
ing grove could undo them all.

"Malum signum."

When he turned his head, he felt the ground scratch-
ing his right eye and tasted repugnant, muddy waters.

"Julio."

Above the noise of the motors and the humming of
tires skimming across the road beyond the fence, he

heard Braulio's voice. He saw him entering the garden, adjusting his nylon windbreaker. He hardly recognized him, covered with that shabby blue garment.

Braulio bent over him. "Julio—what happened?"

"Malum signum," he repeated, clutching Braulio's shoulder. "Malum signum, Braulio, malum."

"Are you sick? Has something happened to you? You're sopping wet."

He made him stand up. Julio took several steps, trying to regain his balance. Leaning on Braulio's shoulder, he went toward the flooded path.

"Let's go to the back of the house."

They went up the fire escape. At the top, the open door was banging, blown by the wind. They went along the shadowy hallway until they came to the lighted library.

"You've got to change your clothes right away, or you'll get pneumonia. What were you doing down there in this weather?"

He went to the bathroom and came back with towels. Julio began to dry his face.

"Go get dressed, please."

Braulio almost had to carry him to the bedroom. "Hurry up, because you're going to get the whole bedroom wet. I don't want to see Luisa's face if she sees us like this. Hurry, Julio, please. You should rub yourself down with alcohol. Cuca says that's the best thing for this. Do you want me to help you?"

"No, no. Better bring me a little rum. See if you can find it. It should be in the library, somewhere you'd never look for it. You know Luisa has a mania for hiding everything."

Braulio left, taking off his jacket as Julio undressed.

He stood naked before the mirror, rubbing himself with the towel to warm up, and dressed, wheezing.

Braulio came back with a bottle and two glasses. "Have a drink."

Julio downed the rum in one gulp and fell exhausted on the bed.

"What happened?"

"I'm all fucked up, Braulio. More than you can imagine."

"But I've told you—please, believe me. Come with me. Let's go see my sister-in-law. She can do something. Why don't we go now? I've got the car outside. I told you I'd come today. She's expecting us."

"I wish I had your faith," Julio cried sadly.

"Then have it, at least through me. Don't you see that they've got your head? They want to drive you crazy. But you have to help the spirits. This whole house smells of magnolias. Your mother planted that tree before she died, and you haven't seen this—look!" He took Julio to the window. "It's the only flower the water and the wind haven't knocked off." He pleaded with Julio. "Believe me. It's a message. They've sent you one message after another and you still don't get it. I've told you a thousand times that Marxism can't explain everything. And I'm sure your dream the other day is an important omen. They're going to call you."

Braulio's face took on its most persuasive aspect, every muscle conspiring to supplicate, appeal to Julio.

"It's possible, Braulio. I don't want to offend you. I respect what you believe; you may be right. But all I know is, I'm completely fucked up." He poured himself another drink and drank it down avidly.

"What about Luisa? Is she still at work?"

"Yes."

"What time does she get home?"

"Today—late, I think. They're going to discuss that project, you know . . . Lately, it's the only thing she can think about."

"So much the better," said Braulio enthusiastically. "Let's go now, we'll be right back. I'll take you."

"All right, then. Let's go."

Braulio's sister-in-law was waiting at the door—an impressive woman, husky, healthy, with a dark complexion and long, strong hair which almost hid her steely eyes and rather fine, smiling lips.

It had been years since Julio had attended one of those rituals—they filled the need for direct dialogue with the dead and the saints, and had become mixed in with the official religions of the country. People had to have those earthly gods who spoke their own language and understood and helped solve everyday problems.

Braulio behaved with respect and reverence. His sister-in-law, her eyes closed, was taking deep breaths, convoking the dead, while he whispered prayers of the Catholic rite, which reached Julio in gusts. Braulio watched him furtively. Suddenly the woman uttered a cry and opened her eyes. Braulio exclaimed, "Mercy!" over and over as she gathered up branches and put them into a pail of water mixed with perfume. She looked at Braulio and asked if he didn't see what she saw. Braulio nodded, exclaiming, "Ave María Purísima!" The woman sprinkled Julio with water and perfume, and turned him around and around while she mumbled unintelligible prayers.

"Leave this body, leave this body! It is not yours!"

She took him by the hands and pulled with great strength, uttering her interminable sputtering whispers. After a while she sat down and asked him to rest on a rough bench in one corner of the room. "They have cast a dark dead man in you, my son."

Braulio nodded.

"We have a big job ahead of us," she whispered.

Braulio wrote down her recommendations: "Honey to protect your eyes from harm, spearmint for health, and rue leaves to break the spell"—an herbarium, really, to counteract his enemies and restore peace and tranquillity. The woman was very moved as she said goodbye; Braulio kissed her on the cheek. As they walked in silence toward the place where they had parked alongside the beach, Julio inhaled that electric, iodine-filled air that had nourished him, weathered him since childhood. In the distance he could see the blinking lights of the fishing boats authorized by the police to fish the open seas, and he knew that other precarious boats were there too, thrown into the flood, making their way through danger, improvised ferries with desperate men and women testing fate daily.

7

EVENING CAME almost suddenly in the wintertime. There
was time only for Ona to notice shadows moving around
her, to smell odors come from the depths of hidden
patios. In near-darkness, she gave herself up to walking.
She had no certain destination; she was led along by the
ineffable charms of the evening. As she walked along the
wide Malecón transformed into a colorless landscape, she
let her mind go over the latest events, one by one: Julio's
disappearance, his frustrated act of love, his agitation,
and that, to her, inexplicable necessity of possession.
She admired a genuine man, tenderly human, incapable
of lying to her, but what was he seeking? Did all Cuban
machos act like that?

It began to rain—not the fine rain of European
winters, but water driven by wind, a tropical cloudburst. Crossing the street on the Malecón in search of
refuge, she was wet through; her clothes clung to her
body and her straight hair trickled water as never before.
She stepped into a wide arcade to catch her breath. At
the other end she saw the barely lit sign of a bar. She
needed a drink; she walked quickly under the colonnade
toward the place she had glimpsed. It was a spacious bar,

with several open doors and, paradoxically, very good light. At that hour of the evening she could sit on a stool and order a rum. Behind her, in a corner, a group of drinkers were improvising songs—a potpourri of guaguancó, bolero, rumba, and mambo. Incomprehensible lyrics, dizzying, repetitive, feverish, and monotonous, were devised to clapping and drumbeats.

Over her shoulder she heard the new, mellifluous voice of a mulatto: "You like music, don't you?" And then, louder: "What are you, Rumanian, Russian, or Polish?"

The Spanish she had learned allowed her to answer with a pleasant smile and a "Why don't you guess?"

But she had mispronounced the words and he corrected her, then asked her name.

The way he spoke seemed funny to Ona. Of course, neither Julio nor Raimundo spoke like that, but she found it nice to know, close up, a real "man of the people," as one of her friends from the commune would say. He was tall and strong, with deeply tanned skin and green, feline eyes. He had a sassy face but it didn't displease her; after all, she was there to corroborate the many versions they sketched of the tropical man, and this one seemed the spitting image of him. He piqued her curiosity. Hadn't the Revolution influenced that brazen gaze at all, that angry mouth, those abrupt gestures? Was a man not the product of his environment? Didn't the Revolution have enough strength to transform this man? Where was the new man? She was going to try to find the answer to so many disquieting questions, but she realized that this was not the most appropriate place. From the corner the songs were like waves washing over her, each one stronger than the last. The group drew a crowd; soon the bar looked almost invaded. The mulatto was no longer talking. He was drinking, too, beside her, never taking his eyes off her. She forgot him for a second, immersed in the mood of the bar. She even felt happy at this feat of hers, at the real possibilities of this incredible night. Now she would really have something to talk about. But to whom? She could talk about these things only to Julio—but where had he gone?

"You look like a little wet chicken, lovely one."

It was the man's voice again. She didn't need to understand his words' meaning; the playful tone of his voice was distinctly erotic. She could only say, "Cubans are very sympathetic."

"Ah, yes? But you don't say sympathetic. Listen, if you want me to, I'll teach you how to say it."

"How, then?"

He gave her the word she wanted, and she repeated it, adding, "Thank you."

"That's better. Well, arrivederci, girl. Take care of yourself."

The mulatto disappeared, and Ona was relieved not to have to make any more effort to talk. She was living through a new experience, and all this was part of it.

She finished her drink slowly. It had stopped raining, and she wanted to go back to her hotel. But when she went to pay, she realized that she didn't have her purse; she remembered having it when she ordered the first drink. Agitated and hardly able to make herself understood, she explained to the waiter.

When she fled from the bar, she was furious with herself. She went to cross the street and heard someone calling her name from a passing car. It was Raimundo, holding something up in his hand—her purse.

"They got the rotten thief in time," he said, getting out of the car, where, tilting her head a little, she could see the now disinterested face of the mulatto. The car sped away.

Raimundo gave her her purse and took her arm. "You shouldn't come out alone to these neighborhoods."

"I thought . . ."

"It's good you thought, but . . ."

Ona roared with laughter. Raimundo, not understanding, decided to wait to lecture her.

"Can you imagine? Can you just imagine?" But she went on laughing. Suddenly she began to cry.

"I don't understand you," said Raimundo, disturbed. "But it'll be better if we go somewhere where you can let this all out. Come on." And he put his arm around her shoulders.

Part Four

"THIS IS THE COROLLARY." Nuria opened the back door of the dormitory and said that the girls here, like him, were prey to unusual emotions, since not a single visitor had found adequate names for them. The brilliant medley of petals and leaves seemed to be shooting off every possible variation of color. Not red, not blue, white, or brown, or black, or gray, but multiple in-betweens—reddish-black, whitish-gray, brownish-blue, bluish-brownish-red-black and red-blue-gray, vibrant colors which gave off auditory and palatal shadings.

The spectacle froze him momentarily dumb. It exerted such fascination that he was incapable even of the suggestion of a gesture or sign of admiration. It was, of course, a wonderland—gravel paths winding along multicolored beds, stone benches in bowers of leaves, trees and branches of every size, and a light that did not shine on the boughs but was everywhere, phantasmal, seeming to emerge from the very roots of the plants.

"Not a single visitor!" repeated Nuria, and added proudly, "It's our garden, and not, as you no doubt think, a miracle of grafting. Grafting doesn't produce

[1 8 3]

miracles, only hybrids do, though we don't dispute its value."

"She means we're not against grafting," another girl put in.

"That's it," Nuria continued. "But our garden has not had the benefit of its advantages. It is"—and here she looked intently at Gregorio—"a *natural* garden. One might even go so far as to say it is exemplarily natural."

"Say it the way you always do, Nuria—naturally natural."

Nuria smiled. But Gregorio heard her words with a mixture of wonderment and shock.

"Naturally natural," Nuria said emphatically. "Oh, don't think we're joking. See over there?"

He couldn't locate the spot in the distance.

"Over there, to the left."

There were flowering rosebushes as tall as she.

"They have a name."

The thirty-six teenage girls assured him in unison that, of course, those roses had been named by the collective, and Nuria asked if he could guess the name. Gregorio said that wasn't exactly what he was best at, guessing, but, urged, he decided to plunge in.

"I . . ." he began.

"Yes, you," they said.

"What would you call them?" Nuria said.

"They're rosebushes, aren't they?" He said it in the doubtful tones people use when the obvious, the all too evident, begins to seem wrong.

"Yes, of course, but you—what would you *call* those roses?"

"I . . ." he said in a slow, soft voice buoyed now by

an almost swaggering certainty, "I would call them Rosaura."

He looked to see what the girls' reaction was, but the thirty-six heads were bowed.

"No," Norma said. "We understand your error perfectly. It isn't the first time. But that never—think of it, Gregorio—it *never* could be the name of these roses."

All the heads nodded at once and he felt like crawling in a hole. He sought Nuria's eyes.

"The name is Conrad," she finally said.

"Yes," sobbed Norma. "Conrad."

"Con . . . oh, yes," chorused the girls.

"But Conrad? Why?" stammered Gregorio. So they told him about the cat, torn to pieces by Frejus.

Frejus was a dog kept by Simplón, a gardener who lived near the camp. It was Norma who told the story, with such vividness that Gregorio saw the shape of the animal menacingly sniffing him—a brown dog, with great striding legs and eyes like lamps. He did not live the carefree life of the camp mastiffs; he was a brawling dog, stealing eggs and killing the camps' gentle, efficient cats. Conrad, said Norma, was not an alley cat, one of those meowing, discontented, lascivious cats that waft along in the wake of female cats. And there were wild dogs and bitches around; one could hear them at night, howling in the hills behind Crucecita or on the coffee plantations in Escambray, frightening the dairy cattle. The cattle were very well protected, but people couldn't keep the dogs from making raids on the other animals in the hills.

Gregorio asked what had happened to Simplón's dog and how Simplón felt.

"Simplón was very sorry. Since then, he's become our

best friend. He tends the garden with us. Thanks to him, we know wonderful secrets for getting those colors."

"And what about Frejus?"

"He ran away. People say they've seen him roaming the outskirts of the camp at night. He better not come back."

"Simplón must have been very upset to lose his dog."

"Well, we loved Conrad very much, too, and now he's dead . . . You have to write about this, Gregorio; it's a beautiful story, our garden and all," said Nuria.

This was the first time Gregorio had ever felt useful in a concrete way. He liked the story of Conrad's garden, he thanked the cat for his immolation—what else could one call it—a death that transformed the cat and proffered Gregorio a wonderful idea. Conrad in many colors, stre-e-etching across the lettering on the book cover, his feet straddling the title, his haughty gray tail making a flourish around Gregorio's name. Children would greet him affectionately in the street. Gregorio felt he'd been resurrected, as a reward for his dedication and hard work.

On the way from camp to the Cienfuegos airport, he imagined the cat in every possible shape, but always somehow insubstantial. He would describe a cat to be admired, respected, loved, which would stir in readers the same love the thirty-six girls had stirred in him. He reserved for Frejus a sententious, angry, pitch-black tar that would make him leap from the pages like a demon. The cover worried him more than anything. He would ask to have a say in it. He dreamed of Simplón's sorrowful eyes, in thick lines, turned toward a Frejus so revolting that he would blot out the reader's natural sympathy for dogs. For this was not man's best friend but the devil's familiar; he would keep, if anything, the large, perhaps redeeming, ears. Nothing else—Simplón looking sadly at Frejus, reproachful, and to one side the innocent, tender Conrad, so suddenly brought to unexpected death.

These images filled his head, but Gloria should know nothing of the project until the end. In fact, he wouldn't write tonight; she would surely become curious and he would feel obliged to tell her the story. This was a piece of good fortune that would reunite them; they would return to the passion of their first years together, to the kisses and caresses of long ago. For that, too, good Conrad had suffered his horrible death.

Gloria didn't hear him open the door or wake up when he cautiously entered the bedroom. She was lying exhausted next to the baby. He gazed tenderly at her; he felt worthy of those two beings who had awaited his transformation with the patience and faith of saints. In the dusk of the bedroom he looked at himself in his work clothes—dusty, sweaty, just emerged from a ditch. He had on a pair of boots that made him several inches taller. He sucked in his gut; finally thin, light, *changed.* He went to the bathroom, took off his clothes, and got under the shower his exaltation had earned him. He stretched out next to Gloria and lay awake a long time, choosing the typeface for the cover, the size he would suggest for his name. He went to sleep thinking of the dedication: "To Gloria, to Jorgito . . . To Gloria, to Jorgito . . ."

"We haven't finished yet. You're still too lazy, Gregorio."

Nuria was before him, haughty and resolute. "You have to come with me. Get up."

Gregorio half opened his eyes. He tried to stammer out some words, but Nuria stopped him. She took his hand, raising him with a light motion that made him float. He more than followed her, he flew with her like a gust of wind. They glided over the garden, in the shadow of the half-moon, and came down on the central esplanade, a perfect landing.

Nuria was panting with excitement. "You still have something to do, Gregorio."

He looked uncomprehendingly at her.

"You don't understand me." She spoke distinctly. "But you should understand me perfectly well. You don't see anything of yours in those trees?"

The air was filled with the perfume of the flowers. Nothing else.

"Nothing?"

"Nothing . . ."

She took him by the arm, leading him through gravel paths and around benches that formed a mad, completely asymmetrical labyrinth. Nuria spun him around on his heels until he was dizzy. And when everything around him had recovered its natural dimensions, he saw nothing but a thick dark woods. Where was that guttural accent coming from, that reiterated command?

"Find it, find it . . ."

He tried to break through the vegetation that fenced him in. There was no path, only many layers of compact vegetation. In a few minutes he was exhausted and fell at the foot of an aged banyan tree, which was replicated in the waters of a broad, smooth lake. The moon shining on the water neatly outlined the tree. He didn't know

this landscape. No one had ever shown it to him before
—but the gravel of the path was not strange to him, or
the cool borders, or the grass, or the branches with
bird's nests, and the rough trunk of the banyan tree
reflected in the water created an almost familiar specter.
The initials etched into the trunk with a knife point,
the intertwined shrubbery encircling him—where in his
memory was there an exact and startling tracing of these
things?

He washed his face at the edge of the water, trying to
revive himself.

"Find it . . ." It was a voice formed of many voices.
Gregorio plunged his head into the water, and when he
lifted it out he discovered the landscape was now tinted
in new shades—reddish, crepuscular. Behind the banyan
tree glowed a flaming horizon. Against the light, the
silhouette of the reclining young man was turned away
from him. He had his hands behind his neck and was
indifferently swinging his boot. The young man didn't
seem to be paying any attention to him, not even when
he was a few steps away. But in a moment he turned
and stood up, tight-lipped, looking about anxiously like
a person chronically perplexed.

This, thought Gregorio, can only be a dream. The old
obsessions, one's adolescence. He had never seen himself
in dreams before. He dreamed of himself or his family
rarely. Most often it was places and landscapes, things
he had been part of, but never with any sense of specific
time or age. And to be in a dream with himself as a boy,
a teenager, the two under the same banyan tree by the
same lake, standing in vegetation which seemed be-
fuddled by the simultaneous presence of the adolescent
and the man—Gregorio felt dizzy, nauseated.

"*Gregorio* . . ." It was his name, but he could not answer. He was immobilized.

"*Gregorio!* . . ." repeated very loud once again; and it was the boy who stood up, brushed the grass from his pants and shirt, and ran off.

He disappeared among the trees, and Gregorio listened carefully to the sounds that indicated which way he went. He walked on and found himself on a stony road, flanked by pine groves that came together in the distance. He couldn't reduce the distance between himself and the boy. Too weak to go on, he fell on his back at the foot of a tree, gasping from exhaustion. Intensely green leaves swayed above his eyes, which were clouded over with perspiration. He breathed in the buzzing, almost palpable air sweeping the pines. After a while he stood up and saw through the tree trunks an old wooden house standing on the slope of a hill, surrounded by tobacco fields. A few paces away was the long, low storehouse with its undulating red plank roof. Gooseberry bushes, soursop, guava, and custard-apple trees, and rachitic, sterile apple and pear trees covered the side of the house; the water barrel was neglected, its tap propped on a large smooth stone. He came closer. The first thing he heard was the sound of the crystal drops of the carbide lamp's fringe stirred by the wind. He entered the deserted house and slipped through the old bedrooms, where a silent unvarying order still reigned.

"First thing—learn to know yourself. These explosions of yours only make you miserable."

The old man smoked his pipe slowly. He talked almost always in the evening, at dusk, when the lamps had not yet been lit and the bees were buzzing in the hives in the orchard. The face of his grandfather, seated on a stool, took on a mysterious hue each time his breathing stirred the pipe's fire.

"We must know our own weaknesses, not just turn them into masks. The brave man is fair, Gregorio. He doesn't seek to rise above his own station. He doesn't try to attain exceptional heights; his own is enough for him." The old man pointed at him with the pipe, in the almost total darkness.

"I don't like to lecture boys; I don't think it does any good. But you worry me. And I know you're going to mull over my advice in your room. And what's more"— he paused, the smoke enveloping him in a reddish cloud —"you like to do compositions, to write. If you keep it up, I predict for you, though I don't wish it, a hard life. Men are mad, Gregorio, and you want to make madmen part of the universe. I read it somewhere—I've often thought it's true. First find out who you are. If you don't try to learn that now, when you're fourteen years old, you'll never learn it. Your life will be a lot of shouting, a struggle, a long suffering."

He went down the steps toward the gravel path; he tousled Gregorio's hair as he passed, and stopped under the arbor at the gate and pulled off a grape and bit it and spat into the darkness.

"You see? Life brings my errors home to me. There is soil that is good for grapes and soil that is not. I'm a man sick with memories, dreaming always about my village in Spain, trying desperately to live *its* geography. I'm a beaten, stubborn old man. I only hang on to my homesickness and a funny kind of old age."

In the house, someone lit the carbide lamp; Gregorio could now see him waving the pipe—his way of underlining his comments. "Whoever doesn't learn in his childhood to know himself won't learn in his youth, and whoever wastes his youth wastes old age, and whoever wastes old age wastes his life. Seek yourself. I don't have much hope, but maybe a blow of some kind will get you to fight and accept. Or confront the end of your own life."

He went toward the house. The moon gleamed on stones and trees. Everything along the pine-bordered path looked silvered, reduced to a single color. He walked hurriedly and then stopped. Nuria came out from among the trees to meet him. He took a few steps.

"Are you running away from me, too?"

"No. But please tell me whether this is a dream or not!"

"That depends on you," Nuria said serenely. "You yourself should decide."

"Cálamus, cálamus, cálamus—" sang Gregorio, affectionately mocking good Panchón, who rocked on his ring, restless but mute. He had learned to repeat the dactyls in the same accent as the parrot. Every afternoon he worked at new phonetic combinations to amaze the group. Gregorio felt happy, with a bursting happiness like a bonfire of freshly cut branches. The dactyls were the crackling of his enthusiasm—his fresh, surprising inventions, a natural explosion of his good spirits. Even his skin had taken on a newborn baby's pinkish tint. The girls noticed it, told him, and he turned his pleased satisfaction to new phonemes and imperatives, which seemed charged with a mysterious immanence. That is, Gregorio changed, and one day seemed to have forgotten the other, the gaunt man that had first come here, pitted, corroded by a spiteful soot. For it wasn't that

Gregorio was altogether another person, but rather that he was now the reference point for himself, the starting point that might serve as an example to other sick people.

He wrote down everything he saw, any time, wherever he was—notes, sketches; and at night, long pages grew out of them.

Gloria hardly knew when he came home, still in the day's work clothes. There were no traces of his having been in the house—the lamp was on till dawn and the pages mounted up, so that it was impossible to conceive that they could have been written in so few hours. He was stealing those hours from his sleep, and Gloria began to fear for his health. But when she saw him come out of the bathroom, his bare chest tanned by the sun, his face eager, without a hint of fatigue or sleeplessness, she was almost reassured. Then, like a girl, she questioned him. He was the traveler returned from the world of fable. What suns, what winds, what grace and wit, what experiences nourished this glorious, untiring man?

He spoke to her of the turbines at the dams and she saw him as part of the cascading water—assigned to it, in its service, sculpted against its headlong clarity. The plantations, which had suffered a prolonged drought, now smiled at this spirited man.

He was always there, among the towers of the oil derricks, his hard hat glinting like a star. He loved this gigantic new world. The gushing oil wet his clothes, jolted him as though it were screaming full in his face.

There were days, weeks, endless months when Gloria listened for his footsteps, heard the key turn in the lock, the door slam, the refrigerator open and close, the water run in the shower, and then almost immediately the hammering of the typewriter, which only stopped at breakfast time, when he mechanically stood up, kissed her, went to the playpen and picked up and petted the baby, gulped down his coffee, and started telling stories as though that were the only possible, expected conversation. Gloria would listen without taking her eyes off him. He was lean, with an impatient light in his eyes, his lips moving passionately, his skin young, fresh; his tangled hair took on the color of its youth. In the tone of his voice she found an innocence, a charm, which contrasted with hers. One morning, watching him change clothes, she saw him naked and she shivered. It was ordinarily she who walked about naked. Now she was terrified that he might uncover her with his gaze, discover her body.

That night, the creak of the bathroom door opening into the room awakened her. In the band of light she saw Gregorio drying himself off as he came naked into the bedroom. He got into bed and lay next to her, and she held her breath, feigning sleep. She felt him caress her slowly and, trying to make him think she was reacting instinctively to his touch, entwined him in her arms. She couldn't stifle a cry of horror—another body, another skin, other hands, another sex joined to hers with a gasping so aggressive that she felt like an old whore, squeezed, used. Roughly, torn between pleasure and shock, she shoved that body away which scarcely needed her to satisfy itself. She sat up on the bed and turned on the light, her sad face in the mirror taking on a mask of age. She stood and brought her face close to the glowing mirror, and, searching in her cropped hair, found some gray strands. She began pulling them out, one by one, breathing harshly, then brushed her hair over and over, breaking into tears as helplessly as a girl.

"What's wrong with you?"

In the strip of light she saw Gregorio, who was drying himself off as he came into the bedroom.

"Nothing," babbled Gloria.

He came near and she jumped away.

"What's wrong, Gloria?"

She took refuge under the blanket, her back to him.

"What's the matter?" he repeated.

She didn't answer.

He pulled her to him and she let him, terrified.

"Something's wrong. You cried out," he said softly.

She remained silent, sobbing weakly.

"Today I was at the ocean," he said after a while. "On the fishing fleet. You should come with me sometime." She said nothing. "Life can be beautiful, Gloria. It is beautiful. I don't understand you, I swear. And what's more," he added vehemently, "you know something? I'm convinced it can transform us and even make *us* beautiful, Gloria. Don't you think that's possible?"

Gloria's uncontrollable weeping drowned out his last words. He kissed her tense lips, her icy breasts, her trembling hands, which she pulled away, defending herself against him.

That night he dreamed of Byelorussia. The guide, a tall thin man with yellowish skin and a shapka pulled down to his eyes and a scarf that hid his mouth when he talked, explained to Gregorio that as he observed the conjunction of the voussoirs that formed the arches, he should pay special attention to the arch stones and the keystone. The arch stones revealed the particular way that that culture conceived the links with the line of horizontal blocks; the keystone showed the angle of the vault with the arris, which joined the two adjoining faces in a way not known in the tropics. When he pronounced this last word, Gregorio discovered the unmistakable accent of lovable Simplón. When he saw that he was found out, he lifted the shapka, behind which gleamed his maddened eyes, and dropped the scarf which hid his mouth, now twisted in a scowl. Gregorio saw, moreover, that he wielded a Russian pistol and was pointing it straight at his face.

"So, a Gothic garden, huh? Well, you're about to die remembering a Baroque one!" he cried, stretching out the *r* of Baroque as though it were a wagon brimming with honey. He blew on Gregorio a breath so strong that he fell among pieces of molding and pediments, trying to fend off the shot with his two hands. He tried to remember words of pleading and absolution, but nothing came to his mind. Then, on the brink of desperation, he cried, "Cálamus, flée from me, pólish me, bánter me"—tattered, incoherent sounds caromed from him off the surfaces of that unknown voussoir.

And he saw Simplón throw down the weapon and take off after his multicolored túrtledoves, their dark-green plumage dappled with black and red spots— smiling like a boy, póinting, rápturous, at the spoon-like flamingo beaks of pélicans and frígate birds, and toucans. He saw him disappear in a dim, impenetrable cloud of dust like a Baroque sentence. He saw him floating, waving to right and left like a man scanning line upon line of poetry, or sprinkling idiotic adjectives over ordinary paragraphs.

He sprang awake. Gloria was asleep next to him. The

baby was curled up at the foot of the bed. A damp, rainy breeze came in through the open window, but he didn't feel like going to close it. So he turned over onto his right side to try to sleep without a nightmare. In a while he glanced toward the window. There was Panchón, sneezing. He was wearing galoshes and a nylon rain cape which clashed with his coat so full of colors that Gregorio imagined him to be a hawker of rainbows. He sat there, with one hand on the windowsill and the index finger of the other in his chattering mouth. Suddenly he shifted from one side of the window to the other as though on a puppet stage. Then he took off his cap and bowed toward an invisible audience, waiting for applause. Finally he sobbed, and what was more curious still, below his wings there were two little violet arms and, at their ends, two little hands that he was anxiously rubbing together.

When Gregorio awoke, the light of day was flooding the bedroom. Through the window he saw the treetops and a clear blue sky. Neither Gloria nor the baby was in the room. The alarm clock showed eight o'clock. He jumped to his feet and went to the bathroom.

While he was shaving, he thought he should pay more attention to his domestic life. No matter how happy you were, you shouldn't disregard the family. And the immediate household problems fell too heavily on Gloria now. How many months had he been neglecting those doubtless minor chores which by their very triviality were nasty and a bore?

He was immersed in these thoughts when he heard a familiar voice coming from the living room. Gloria was trying to explain things to the head of personnel in her company. How could she leave the baby alone? She had no one to help her. Not a sister, or a cousin. Just two old aunts, in their eighties, with arthritis and heart disease, whom she visited once a month. She couldn't count on Gregorio. She didn't even want to suggest it to him. He didn't want demands of any kind. Gregorio needed all his time.

The personnel manager spoke calmly, but he was in a difficult situation. Her case would have to be brought to an immediate solution; that was the only thing to do.

"I don't understand it," the personnel manager repeated. "Believe me, Gloria, I don't understand it at all."

She made no effort to explain further; she simply stated that it was impossible for her to take on the burden. Gregorio's work came before everything else. She had powerful reasons not to leave him at that moment.

"I am very sorry," she said. "I'm very sorry, but that is my situation."

Above the conversation, he heard the baby's gurgling. Through the half-open door, Gregorio saw the man looking puzzled at Gloria.

He went on watching, still drying his face, as though his eyes were beginning to see a new reality. Even Gloria looked different, with her black hair just combed, her blue jeans with a white blouse tucked into them. He saw her let the personnel manager out, close the door and release a sigh, and walk to the playpen, where the baby bounced up and down with pleasure at having her so near.

She took a metal top and pressed the handle so it went

spinning across the wooden floor of the playpen. A tune he didn't recognize came out of it. Jorgito watched the toy with a smile of satisfaction. Then Gregorio went to her.

"Who were you talking to?"

"The personnel manager came by. He wants me to go to work as soon as possible. I told him I couldn't just now. We won't be able to put the baby in a nursery until September. They simply have to wait. But they're impatient. Are you going to have breakfast?"

She went to the kitchen and got him his breakfast. Gregorio sat down at the table, facing her. She was still upset.

"Well, I'm sure they must need you."

"There are hundreds of people that can do what I do," she said.

"But maybe they need *you*, Gloria."

"Well, it isn't the moment, even if I wanted to."

When he finished eating, he said, "The best thing is to make arrangements for you to go back as soon as possible . . ."

She interrupted him. "It would be at the cost of your work."

"No, it wouldn't."

"Yes, it certainly would. And the most important thing now is your work. What you're doing *is* important; it won't be me that keeps you from it."

He smiled softly. "It's a matter of getting up more steam. I'll try."

"No, Gregorio. You need all this time and more." She squeezed his hands. "I want you to work and win," she added with emotion. "It's really the only thing that matters to me. That you win. That you show you can rebuild your life, that it's always possible to start again, that you're not—you're not desensitized, Gregorio."

She had tears in her eyes. "You've changed so much, Gregorio. You've lost weight, you look younger. You look adjusted. Me, though . . ." She couldn't go on. She began to cry again, as she had the night before.

"I don't understand what's wrong with you," he said in a voice that seemed to Gloria to be that of a troubled child.

"You aren't the same, Gregorio. Don't you see that you're absolutely not the same? That you're another man, completely different?"

2

HE YANKED the paper from the typewriter. He tore it to pieces. He sat down, exhausted and sweating heavily. He opened the terrace windows. A thick warm wind rushed into the room, scattering the recently written sheets of manuscript. He mentally repeated the last line, "Who can I be? Who can I be?" as though it were addressed exclusively to him. While he poured himself a drink from the almost empty bottle, he repeated the question aloud.

"For the moment, still a drunk," he heard someone answer behind him. He turned around, startled. Gloria was beside him. She tried to grab the bottle, but he dodged and swung it like a baseball bat. She stopped him, irked.

"Do you mean to tell me you're capable of throwing that bottle into the street? Put it wherever you want to, but try not to act like a case for a padded cell." Her voice had a dull, beaten tone. Gregorio put the bottle on the desk and went toward the terrace, trying to keep his balance. Then he fell into one of the chairs, panting, his face turned to the bay. It was vibrant, red in the sunset. The light brought his cheekbones into relief; his eyes were bloodshot and his hair tousled and sweaty.

"I wish you could see yourself in the mirror now. You look like a street urchin."

He turned sharply, trying to make a gesture of reply on his fuddled face.

"Why did you tear up that page? Why are the rest of the pages scattered all over the floor?"

She sat down by him, at his feet, as she had done so many times before; she squeezed his arm.

"Leave me alone," he cried, and covered his face with his hands.

"Have you been writing all these hours so everything would turn out the same as before, a pile of scattered pages, unnumbered, that you hide like a stigma?"

"Leave me alone, please."

"Are you going to tell me again that you didn't like them? You don't like them, isn't that right? They're not up to your standards. No page is worthy of you. You're a genius. Everything you do has to be dazzling, peerless. That's why you don't want to show me what you write. You don't want me to find out you've scratched it all out a thousand and one times, or that you made a mistake and wrote something ambiguous, which you can't stand, or put down images that piss you off."

She paused, then blurted out: "Well, I've read it all. Everything you've written and then stashed away. I've found it and read it all, do you hear?"

"No!" he shouted.

"All these pages you've been hiding from me—like a miser with his hoard."

"No!"

"Whole chapters covered with blotches and scribbles. Paragraphs marked over and over with a red pencil."

"Liar!" he cried, his voice beaten, wavering.

"I've read them with a magnifying glass to see what word you wrote the first time. I know your tricks now, Mr. Writer."

She stopped, gauging the shattering effect of her words on that torn face. He was trembling all over; his eyes were filled with tears like a boy's; even his voice took on the helplessness of his childhood.

"Tell me that's not true, you haven't been going through them, Gloria, please."

"I have, I'll go on doing it," she said slowly and deliberately, "and I should never have let it be any other way. Every day, I want to read what you've written, and discuss it with you."

He leaned back in the chair with his eyes closed. She stroked his hand, kissed it. There was silence for a few minutes. It had turned night, and now only twinkling lights could be seen, scattered on the wide expanse of the bay. From the street came the muffled sounds of traffic, diminishing with the hours. The wind had begun to slacken, to take on the cool dampness of spray. After a while he said, "You came to the conclusion that I'll never be able to do anything that's any good, right?"

"I like your ideas, your economy of means, your desire to mix reality and imagination, dream; but that double of yours, who's almost you anyway, seems nauseating to me."

"Never anything worthwhile, right?"

She went on without listening to him, absorbed in her own reflections. "He's an egoist, willfully sick. He's always examining himself, as though he were the center of the world."

"Pages and pages of culls, pure shit, isn't that right," he cried, pulling his hand away. "A tedious technical exercise going nowhere—words and more words, and nothing behind them. Why don't you tell me so? Do you feel sorry for me?"

"I said I like your idea and your development. I like the fact that it's a novel that cancels itself out as it goes along, and keeps being born from its own destruction. A writer wants to reflect a world in transformation that runs ahead of him and makes him face up to his own deformities, defects, vices. He struggles to overcome them by an iron discipline—I like that—but a drunk loaded down with morbid memories, always on the outside of things and people, who never goes inside to live as they do, with them, seems absolutely nauseating to me. If you want to set up a conflict between memories and the present, at least don't let memories prevail. Don't make a monument to nostalgia and melancholy. You have to drown that past, bury it inside yourself. Living with memories is lovely; but living *on* them, feeding on them, is a kind of death. Let all this remembering go, Gregorio. That past doesn't exist anymore, understand? Begin by telling yourself that none of that exists anymore, that everything is quite dead. It's no more than an image in your memory, and you let it torture you. You'll never be able to describe exactly how it was."

Ten years before, as he crossed the Borodino Bridge in the snow, wrapped in the heavy Russian overcoat, with the earflaps of his cap loose in the frozen wind, his steps creaking on the white ground of Smolenskaya Nabreznaya, he had been sure that one day he would describe it exactly as it was. With the years, when experiences and voyages had blurred out the superfluous, he would close his eyes and enter the great city again as he had the first day. Nothing had been erased by time.

That first winter he had lived alone in his apartment in Smolenskaya. Tatiana would come in at noon. She appeared first in the square of the window—broad and solid, with boots and overcoat and head scarf standing out black against the drifts of snow piled up all over Moscow. She would knock softly on the door and come in, greeting him in the same tone of voice, in the same mood as always. After a while she would bring in a cup of steaming tea for each of them. She would drink hers in silence. He would look at her cheeks reddened by the winter, her small round eyes intensely blue, her wispy short graying hair. After they drank the tea, she would take away the cups, and in a while he would hear her sweeping the floor of the apartment.

In the evening, before she left, he would invite her to have some Armenian cognac and ask her to tell him of the hard times of her youth in the October Revolution. It was that humble side of the epic that she placed in his remembering. The years '17, '19, '23 took on life in her serious, often hoarse voice. Then she talked to him of the Great War that she had lived through during the apex of her life. Her children had died at the front at Stalingrad, but her husband had survived all catastrophes. "What's left are the old burned tree trunks," she would say.

After drinking 150 grams of cognac—the limit she set

for herself—she wrapped herself up as she had been when she came in and he saw her retrace the path, choosing the same stretches, skirting the same obstacles, crossing the same bridge over the same snowy river.

Now Gloria was asking him to drown that past. Him, who had strained to hold on to the least details, the most imperceptible impressions, she asked him to bury it within himself, to erase it all.

And likewise to bury within himself, erase, the human alluvium that mingled together every morning in the various metro stations in Moscow. It was an active, silent multitude whose fates, longings, worries, and dreams were expressed in their frank, open faces. He sought in every physiognomy the traces of war and struggle, but they were all infused with serenity and simplicity instead, and this impressed him deeply. These were things he thought about at night, in his room, for long hours before he went to sleep. He dreamed of describing that fascinating world one day as neatly as he saw it, bathed by no distorting, sickly light. Did it impress Gloria as a desolate world because he blurred the real images? And if he did, what did he blur them with? What stubborn intermediary substance adhered to them? Was it that their evocations came from a man who now could never again contemplate that world at close range?

Gloria was proposing that he work a little more on concrete, immediate life, leaving memories behind. She asked him to have his character show that he was trying to internalize the world he lived in, his time, his people. Romantics were notoriously incapable of getting out of themselves. Every writer is tempted to take unhealthy pleasure in himself. One has to allow other situations, other characters to come into close range. One has to abandon fable—so his convictions told him. "You can do it. Forget you and me. We aren't important. What's important is this writer you've conceived. Work on him."

Suddenly the phone rang in the living room and Gloria stood up. "I'll be right back," she said, and went to answer it.

Gregorio bowed his head and put the Borodino where it belonged, in his memory. A gypsy couple were sitting there, singing ballads in the Kiev station, a few steps from the bridge. They were drinking old vodka, and since he was the spectator most moved by their songs, the gypsies passed him the bottle to drink, as a sign of friendship. He drank again in memory, and down his throat flowed the old strong taste. Snow began to fall so compact and constant that one could hardly see a yard away, and the slightly tremulous voices unexpectedly took on a totally unreal resonance. He remembered the hands that passed him the bottle through the whiteness, as the wind made whirls of snow around them.

It was snowing when he arrived in Moscow. It often snowed when winter began to deepen, and now there was only that huge whiteness which cast its glow against the night and still was casting it in his memory.

But now he was convinced that that landscape was lost forever, and something equally grave—his memory was a fun-house mirror, another symptom of his sadness and despair.

He had an urge to drink, to drink long, to dilute that trance of torturing lucidity. He closed his eyes and walked again through the snowy city. He walked very slowly, with a horror that he would lose or confuse the tiniest detail. He began with Pushkin Square. He retraced Gorky Street several times, inch by inch. He did it at different times of day. He sat down in the little park by the Aragay Restaurant, till midnight. Then he walked toward the Hotel Moscow, and when he was certain that he would remember down to the brand of the Bulgarian cigarette butts that accumulated in the enormous brass ashtrays, he decided to go on foot to Arbat Street, and from there again to Borodino. He took off his gloves and lovingly pressed the handfuls of snow that fell, slow, over the hard white river. A few yards away rose the skyscrapers of Moscow, all identically constructed. Along the banks slid the thin traffic of that hour. He contemplated it all again as though it had been a maquette patiently built up in his heart. Then, without anyone seeing him, he vanished.

From the living room he seemed to hear Gloria's smiling voice mingling with other voices, other men's and women's laughter. He stood and went into his study. Now he heard only Gloria.

"I think one has to keep his promises, isn't that right?"

The visitors agreed. He figured out that there was a man and two women; but he couldn't place their voices. Gloria went on telling them that a man who can't keep his promises isn't worth a fig. She added that, if she hadn't pushed him, he wouldn't have accomplished a thing. She wasn't completely satisfied; the whole business was still too unstable; she had to underline that, it was very important. They should keep it in mind, because that's what they had come for today.

He went into the bathroom and got under the shower. He came out almost immediately, dried himself off, and put on clean pants and a shirt. He couldn't find his shoes. He put on some sandals that were pretty old but still looked all right.

"But he is keeping his promise. Within the bounds of possibility, of course, but he is keeping it."

Gloria was speaking resolutely and happily, which contrasted with the asperity and pushiness of only a few moments ago.

"I suppose you want to see him right away, don't you?"

The laughter advanced toward the terrace. Gregorio quickly combed his hair, tucked in his shirt, and checked himself in the mirror. Then he went out to the terrace. He was just about to sit down, when he heard the laughter suddenly cease and Gloria's voice become low and whispering. Moments later, she came alone toward him. "Gregorio."

He glanced up at her. "What's wrong? What are you up to? Who's there? Didn't someone phone?"

"It was a wrong number. I have a surprise for you," she said, smiling mischievously. "A real surprise."

"What's all this about? Tell me."

"There's somebody to see you."

"I know somebody came. Who?"

"A visitor you have to see," added Gloria.

"Gloria, please, stop this game now."

"Norma is here."

Gregorio looked at her, incredulous. "She's come with Nuria and Panchón."

❧ 3 ❧

THE FIRST ONE to get out of the car was Nuria; then Panchón and Norma, slamming the doors. Gregorio walked ahead of them, docilely, as though they were all ruled by an old design. Neither Gloria nor the child could deflect a mandate anterior to their tiny lives. They didn't speak a word, they simply walked on. Gregorio heard the creak of their soles on the gravel of a walk which kept changing—first into paving stones, then cobblestones, that he, with a languid smile, could describe.

"I'm sure the bridge comes next." He suddenly saw it, swallowed in fog, a bridge that grew not as in dreams but like the simple extension of a real project. The sky, high above, showed signs of a storm. Gregorio felt the prodigious relief of a man who has been freed from all indeterminacy and surprise. Before him opened a wide esplanade, and at the precise corner that nothing and no one could alter, he saw the two men—dark suits, caps pulled down across their brows, and an almost touching easiness of manner. The foreseen end. The first to throw herself on him, sure and quick, was, of course, Nuria. Panchón and Norma finished her work, prisoners, too, in the grand design.

"It's true that the strongest blow generates its own negation, its own anesthesia," gasped Gregorio.

Every plot, every invention must end in the same way. There is no chance even in the most forced fantasy—it is right that in every plot there should be reciprocal victims. Jejune thoughts, he told himself. Even in this, you outdo yourself, exceed yourself, become so much hot air. He didn't try to look once more, not even for just an instant, at the pebbled walk, the medieval bridge Norma, Nuria, and Panchón were walking away on. Why waste time? He was now residue, spectacular nothing.

Reciprocal victims that we invent, or that invent us. You pay the price one way or another. It was then the knife appeared. How many heads of the contemporary imagination had that bright blade passed through, that razor conceived in an old city of fogs? That timid, quiet little man chained to the only metaphor of his only life, swallowed like everyone else by that fog, pierced by the same horrors, victim to his own invention, his own sorcery.

"Like a dog," said one of the men as he buried the knife in Gregorio's breast.

Why? It was a commonplace no one had ever dared question. Die like a dog, live like a dog, screw like a dog in heat. Why that irrational vilification substituting for the virtue of loyalty a stream of crude abuse?

Gloria's tenacity, the baby's happiness could do little. People fall apart, they can't go on, they are suddenly shattered like ancient shells of buildings, even if they were made of concrete. The best metaphor for life is death; they are woven together to make the braid. They live by their very distance from each other. Sentences for the end of a chapter, the language fatally pompous. But that little man, the virtual amanuensis of a precise terror, hadn't talked like that. Put no fire in anything; blow, animate no life in anything. The new, perhaps the only, vitality—there are the hopeful ruins, the vital undone crowns, every day, stirring as at an uncontrollable birth. It might be that true ardor resides at the heart of crisis, in the endless cycle of destruction and renewal from disasters.

"For the end of a chapter," the ceremoniously bowing man said, the man who buried the blade in his breast.

"Like a dog."

An end, however it came. His end. He didn't want to argue with them. Nuria, Norma, and Panchón would be of the same mind as Gloria. Piled-up pages whose only purpose had been to catalogue simple bitterness. An effort, a labor damned beforehand, a mediocre show of recuperation. Let others tell what he wasn't able, didn't know how, to tell, let someone else put ear, eye, to the epic. He didn't feel like arguing. So he left them, excused himself, or tried to, and went into the street. It was futile for Gloria to call him over and over. For Norma, Nuria, and Panchón to look on, perplexed. "Gregorio!" they called, but he didn't come back.

The din of the bar swept over him like a cloud of smoke; he took it all in as though it were a natural place. People continued doing what they were doing, no one looked at him when he went up to the bar and ordered a double *añejo*. The sudden effect of the rum, that fiery current entering his bloodstream, seemed to wrap him in a sheet of flame; he drank a second and a third; the pleasant softness produced by alcohol was washing over him. The bartender held up the bottle and looked at him, expecting him to ask for another.

"Okay, the next one," but he drank this one slowly, turning the glass in his hands.

"Like a dog." A commonplace that involuntarily coincided with greatness, as Camus said of the last words of the dying Rimbaud. Only genius implies virtue, not renunciation of genius. He wasn't so sure now. That pronouncement was pompous, too. It could be focused in another way, as well. No more virtue, the word which betrayed and turned arrogant in view of the fragility of men's lives. Virtue? He smiled. When we begin to doubt the noblest things, we don't become better for it, we trace the design of our own ruin. For the end of a chapter. A chapter of what? What capitulation might it effect, what would it culminate, even just finish up? He drank the last sip and began to study the bar, as he had done years before.

In the bar there were so many illusions, that is, words, which rose up before him. Before, he had seen everything as a function of literature; the happiest beings, tattered and weakened people were all joined for him in an identical glistening web. Those lives, plots, were the core of his faith, his reason for being. Had he really seen them, though? There they all were, there, in that dirty café full of smoke and shouting—gesticulating, letting themselves go—drinking, wiping themselves out, opening their hearts to each other.

The door of the bar opened and closed. He looked attentively at the people who came in; they came in drunk. Soon he recognized Julio but tried to pretend he hadn't. But Julio came straight up to him and put a hand on his shoulder. Gregorio turned.

"Hi."

"Hi. Have a drink."

"Okay, but I'm buying."

He didn't let him order.

"Really. I want to buy you a drink," Julio insisted. "I *need* to buy you a drink."

Gregorio looked uncomprehendingly at him. "Why exactly do you *need* to?" He sketched a light smile. "Maybe it's me who needs to."

They had several drinks, both of them drinking to forget. After a while Julio said, "I think we're a little counterproductive here. In all these years, this is the first time we've *really* faced each other."

"We've seen each other, I guess, but this is really the first time we've met."

"Well, it's that everything, everybody is so complicated," Julio said.

"And on the defensive, too."

"We live just a few steps from each other and only see each other go in and out."

"Not everybody is like that. People meet and talk."

"Not us."

"Those old people—are they friends of yours?"

"Not friends—I don't think that's hard to guess."

"Just a manner of speaking. Let's drink up."

They had another drink.

"Why have we run into each other here? Isn't it incredible? All these years living practically next door, and all of a sudden we meet here. I think your wife'll be the first one to be surprised when she hears."

"*If* she hears."

"You aren't going to tell me she won't notice you came home plastered. Women smell alcohol a mile away."

"In that case, maybe she'll notice." He paused for a long time, then finally said, "I'll drink to the roof falling in. I'll drink to my own ruin."

A different Luisa appeared before him, the furious creature squeezed into the old tailored suit, throwing in his face everything she had been storing up for so many years, things he perhaps himself had planted in her—but Gregorio Suárez didn't know this, his surprise at seeing Julio didn't take this in. He raised his glass to drink to ruin. He was tight, his eyes were bloodshot, and his tongue was clumsy and thick. He said, "To ruin," and drank.

"Why ruin?" Julio asked. "You could drink to more certain monstrous disasters."

"You said it," cried Gregorio.

"To the future that kills us, to the models of the perfect future which will make us a sinister memory— to the cities of the sun that will burn us to a crisp, to Sir Thomas More, and Morris and Fourier and all the orthodox utopians who dream of cities no one will ever live in."

"If you drank to the ideal world, what would it be?"

"To a world of one-eyed, homosexual, alienated, desperate men—to a world simple and real."

"To a new Noah's ark," Gregorio cried.

"To any old deluge, any real past. To no hope . . . What would you drink to?"

[2 1 5]

"To what I *do* drink to."

"What do you do besides type all the time? Don't tell me you're an informer, like Fernández Junco says."

"Maybe they are reports, in a way, but there's not a one you won't find my own downfall written into."

"What the hell is it you do?"

Gregorio looked fixedly at him. Then he said, "A book. A novel."

Julio burst out laughing, but he drank to all the pages and chapters, to what he had saved and what he had thrown out, to the plot and to the characters.

"Well then, what novel do you want to write?"

"A long stupid story of love, to make people happy and make them cry."

"That deserves a double," Julio cried.

And they drank a double. Gregorio's eyes blinked heavily and Julio realized the man was wiped out. He thought they'd better leave before they attracted too much attention. Gregorio wouldn't listen. He said again, "A fable, a long sad tale."

"That's a criticism of the world's nostalgia."

"No!" Gregorio said. "Criticism of nothing! I want imperishable bliss. I love the world's duration—its existence is its glory. Let pestilence, plagues, the tiny joys of the world as it *is* be immortal. We should drink a toast to the people who write those new gothic romances now, to immortal fertile tears."

Julio agreed, but as he looked toward the end of the bar, he discovered that other eyes were watching them. Constant witnesses.

"Let's go somewhere else," he said. "I've got the car outside."

Before he left, Julio bought a bottle of Ronda, which

the bartender handed him wrapped in a newspaper. It was getting dark, and as he was getting into the car, Gregorio almost tripped into one of the many puddles covering the sidewalk. The great trees of the Quinta Avenida threw their little fugitive fans of rain against the windshield each time the breeze stirred the branches. The wonderful, almost cold, breeze, the sudden and restorative gift of certain nights of the Cuban December, a deceptive month, inklings of motion in a temperature that the Gulf waters didn't ever really allow to reach the island, made entirely of sun, humidity, and greenness.

Gregorio fell into the front seat and Julio opened the door, but the clear, cool, starry night held him a second. He looked at it as a man might look at a beautiful yet sinister thing.

"I'd like to describe you, enchanting vastness. I'd like to give you a name, but it would just be words." The iodized breeze flooded his lungs, wrapped him in a thick oleaginous mass. The breeze of the tropics.

But his frontiers now spread. "I'd like to go swimming now, underwater, touch some distant coast, no history." An ancient time, absolute, petrified, but a time that demanded no participation from him, no dream, no nightmare. There were moments he dreamed of tremulous ferries that could carry one without any moral demands. One could love this great, warm, measureless island; but right now all he wanted was to flee from it, obliterate a dream that for him had become a nightmare. Diderot, when he wrote about Seneca, agreed with him in the formulation that only certain very specific experiences can produce: "There is a moment when people do not wish to order or to obey, only to escape."

❧ 4 ❧

GROGGY, driving solely by reflex, Julio passed the bay tunnel to East Havana and headed down the wide, four-lane highway with its median lined with mercury lamps—the lights burned out every little stretch. Air different from Old Havana's, clean and morning-like, blew through the pines. He crossed through one of the narrow toll lanes which until 1960 had been manned by uniformed toll collectors nimbly taking in dimes; the car barely slowed, and again entered the highway, which flowed grandly beside the open, glittering sea.

He drove past the blocks of workers' dwellings beside the Naval Hospital, crossed under the pedestrian bridges that linked the asphalt paths on each side of the central roadway in a half-finished architectonic tracery—all of it now covered with weeds so thick the asphalt of the streets and the concrete sidewalks barely showed through. There were only a few houses scattered irregularly across the great abandoned expanses.

Between Cojimar and Alamar he let the car's impetus carry him into a residential neighborhood. The narrow street was covered with loose asphalt gravel, the tires popped; at one of the potholes he lost control of the steering wheel and ran into the grassy ditch. Branches whipped at his face through the window.

Gregorio raised his head. "What's happening?" He spoke drunkenly.

Julio got the car under control. Gregorio fluttered his eyes and repeated the question.

"Nothing, buddy."

Julio went on between the rows of dark houses, which foreign technicians lived in. The car lurched over the bumpy ground and stopped almost at the water's edge, on the rocky, sandless beach. The winter sunrise was a pale line on the choppy waters.

Julio got out, trying hard to keep his balance.

"What's happening?" Gregorio insisted, not quite awake.

"We're drunk as lords. Get out. I'm going to take a little dip."

Gregorio protested. "It's cold. I'm not going swimming."

Julio stripped naked. The cool air made him shiver. Then he got the bottle of rum, took a long pull and ran toward the sea. The shock of the water made his temples explode. He stayed for a few seconds inches from the bottom before he came up to the surface and began to swim smoothly, with a sensation of coolness and heaviness. His body wanted to feel light, and so, with powerful strokes, it tried to buoy itself up. He dived again, and scraped the ocean bed with his hands. Then he surfaced and swam toward shore. Gregorio was sitting naked, drinking next to the car.

"Come on, jump in."

Gregorio ran toward a promontory rising up from the shoreline. "Man overboard!!" He did a booming belly dive onto the water, sank, and reappeared, gasping, exhausted. "It's like ice."

"Only at the beginning. Start swimming."

"I can't," he gasped.

"Well, try."

He made a few clumsy strokes, but his motions betrayed him.

Julio swam toward him. "Float, then."

He floated on his back, breathing anxiously. "I'm beat."

"You're drunk."

"*We're* drunk."

"You're drunker than I am."

The light grew stronger on the horizon; the gray waters now took on the colors of day.

"You have to do it yourself. Try to make for shore."

Gregorio turned over and swam, but he didn't get far.

"It's only a little ways more."

Julio dived for the last time and opened his eyes in the now translucent water. The seabed looked muddy, with long stretches of rocks covered with seaweed and sea urchins. A few fish dizzyingly darted across his line of vision. Julio stayed down until he felt the pressure in his ears and then went back up. The morning light brought out the swells and the rocky design of the coast and its houses. When he turned, he saw Gregorio adrift, struggling to keep himself afloat. Julio swam toward him and grabbed his hair to try to tow him toward the beach. At the boggy edge of the water, Julio raised his head and lightly slapped the pale, swollen face. Then he pumped his arms, giving Gregorio artificial respiration, until Gregorio finally gasped, his eyelids fluttering open. Julio dragged him farther up and managed to prop him against the promontory. He went to the car and brought back the bottle of rum and began to rub his arms and body.

"Drink this. Drink a little."

"Cramp."

"Drink a little. Drink—we've got to go. It's almost daylight. We're out here stark naked and all those foreign technicians live right over there. Hurry up."

Gregorio drank the rum and unsteadily got to his feet.

"You want me to rub your legs?"

"No. Don't waste the rum."

Along the highway, just a few yards from them, they heard the purring of an engine.

"Hurry up, somebody's coming."

They ran toward the car. Behind the houses, men's and women's voices could be heard singing work songs out of tune, and the sound of the engine coming closer.

"A couple of fags! Look, a couple of fags!"

At first there were voices and guffaws; but suddenly a deep angry voice cried, "Get 'em!"

"How disgusting!" women shrieked.

"Queers!" cried the frenzied chorus.

Stones fell near Julio. Gregorio tried to pull on his pants, and a rock bounced against his back.

"Don't worry about getting dressed. Get in or we're screwed."

Gregorio jumped into the car and Julio revved the engine.

The voices got louder and louder, angrier and angrier, stones banged against the roof and doors of the car. Julio floorboarded the accelerator and the car spun along the gravel road until it got back up onto the highway.

"Watch your head."

Heberto Padilla

He tried to avoid potholes, though his foot was still holding the accelerator to the floor; the thick branches along the abandoned stretch of road whipped the windshield. Gregorio had his head down, still clutching the bottle of rum.

"See if they're following us."

"I don't think so. I don't see anything," said Gregorio, looking all around. Before coming to the Via Blanca, Julio turned down a road of mangrove trees which went toward the ocean.

"Let's go—step on it!"

"I know where I'm going!" shouted Julio, slowing down.

The road came out on the beach, where they smelled the stagnant water of the mangroves. Suddenly the vegetation gave out and a rocky esplanade appeared, almost bare, with a few palm trees scattered irregularly across it. The brightness of the day gave the gigantic waves a reddish nimbus; the golden haze of sea spray was as high as the mangroves.

Julio drove on slowly, avoiding rocks, but when he tried to park on one side to hide the car among the trees he felt the engine sputter. He stepped on the starter again but he couldn't get the motor going.

Gregorio looked anxiously at him. "What is it?"

"Either it's overheated or worse, I don't even want to think about it, maybe it's out of gas."

"You think so?"

"We'll wait a while. This car overheats sometimes."

"Don't flood it. Let it alone for a minute." He handed him the bottle. "Have a drink. We were saved by a miracle. Can you imagine what would've happened to us?"

x

[222]

Julio took a drink and gave him back the bottle, which Gregorio immediately lifted to his mouth.

"Don't drink so much. You're sloppy drunk already," cried Julio, snatching the bottle away.

"One more," Gregorio said.

They had another, but the sticky humidity wasn't dispelled by the alcohol. The wind made them shiver, even in the closed car.

Julio stepped on the starter again, but the motor gave only a weak, sputtering noise. Then he pressed the accelerator several times to prime the carburetor, and, his foot tense on the pedal, turned the key. The engine suddenly started. Julio kept pumping until the car was running smoothly. He put it in first and drove along the road bordered by palms.

"They had us by the balls," said Julio, cupping his crotch as though for protection. "If the car hadn't started, we were screwed." But when he turned to look at Gregorio, he saw Gregorio's head slumped on his chest. He was asleep. He shook his shoulder, but Gregorio only uttered a groan of protest.

Julio looked around. The coast was completely deserted. Through the mangroves, frightened herons were crisscrossing, little black birds fled through the branches; a few iguanas and ferrets skittered over the swampy land. In a few minutes the sun would be completely up; even now, the light illuminated half the sky, canceled shadows. The water glittered intensely; waves were breaking against the cliffs and shattered into millions of drops, forming a salty, trembling veil-like mist. Then, the motor still running, Julio sat back in the seat and rested his head against the seat back, his eyes closed. The last twenty-four hours loomed like a nightmare through which he floated, naked and dripping wet from the muddy water he had waded in. Luisa—had she gone back home? He imagined how uneasy she'd be that he was so late. Humberto would tell her, anyway, or Braulio or Cuca. But had she really gone back? Had she clung to Gloria and cried on her shoulder, the way women do after a breakup? He wondered where Luisa was now. And Ona? It was strange, Ona was a dim memory. Luisa held the center of his anguish, as though the last painful meeting with Ona had not been, as though the ridiculous consequences of the last meeting had broken him free of her. All he had now was the image of those first days—their conversations, during their walks, about the plans for the development of the Revolution, her enthusiasm, her unwavering security, her optimism, her open happiness. Everything came back to him, neatly, like the lines of her face. She would be catching the plane now, or maybe not. Perhaps on the way to the airport, escorted by the guide on duty (who?), perhaps sitting in the room at Protocol, making the last hurried notes so she wouldn't forget a single detail of her visit. How would he appear in her book? An architect stuck between two epochs, a superseded conscience, a petit-bourgeois professional homesick for a life abroad, a skeptic, a sentimental goose, an obtuse liberal, a cynic? What would his name be, there in that black notebook where she wrote in a crabbed, agitated calligraphy?

"You should all have your necks wrung," Luisa had shouted at him hours before. Not because she really thought so. She was no more radical or lucid than he in political matters; she shared his unsureness. And, though for different reasons, she reacted in the same way he did. But the fact that she used a political argument to reproach him for his conduct with Ona showed that the country's political tensions had crept into everything—they hung over everything, dominated every life, got into the mouths and subconsciousnesses of everyone. Not even the breakup of a marriage was free of their taint—her fierce accusation was irrefutable, like a prejudice that erupts when one least expects it. Politics fired the last argument of all friends; it furnished the only pretext which legitimized breakups and quarrels. Luisa had also adopted that argument, she worked that vein well—she saved herself by throwing it up to him—she exorcised and transformed herself by accusing him of being an enemy of the Revolution. How many people had he seen resort to such words during the last few years? That was not a sign of people's convictions, or of the evolution of political consciousness; it was a mark of compliance or resignation. When people went over to the system, they started life anew, took out a safe-conduct pass through the future, made a comfortable adjustment, as though going through a school graduation at which diplomas are given out and suddenly all the bad grades, failed exams, misconduct are canceled, for that diploma carries the power of birth or resurrection. Even the professors we hate or who hate us feel relief when it is granted us, because it is a sanction for burying old antagonisms and disputes. Lapsed Catholics who months before were totally damning the system came to it with such ease that it was as though the old dogma had changed its meaning.

They manipulated the new slogans with the devotion they had had before for prayers; they repeated them with the vehemence of a sacramental mystery-play, of a profession of faith. They were not reproached for their old beliefs and attitudes; those were locked into a filing cabinet to be opened only in an extreme emergency, and daily obedience could almost always cancel them out. Backslider and counterrevolutionary, bourgeois and beatified, all changed; years of wear and fatigue authorized, morally *demanded* change.

Had Luisa signed up along with the crowd of new converts? Had she finally tired of a rebellion that brought nothing but anguish and desolation?

Perhaps it was true, perhaps this ability to change was not reproachable, but was, rather, the only possible choice, the only road. History was slow . . . and cruel. Man's limited judgment could not mitigate it. What am I doing, throwing up moral demands against a movement that passed its protagonists by, made them victims or hangmen? The only thing that's real is the danger of a restoration, as Humberto said; the important thing is to resist, to stand up to difficulties and frustrations, to try to promote the healthiest course. On that shore, everyone was swimming as Gregorio had been a moment ago. "Only I see a difficult path, only I see indecency; I am the one who is obscene." In his boyhood he had gotten the saints mixed up and prayed to one and another indiscriminately; he gave frog's feet to his guardian angel and huge wings to the insipid apostles in the lithographs, and this confusion had begun to nourish his disillusionment as before it had fed his faith. If he had lost it, who cared? His despair was not linked to the world, it was a kind of visceral, organic abnormality, and sick men don't make history.

He turned, furious, to Gregorio and shouted at him to wake up, wake up, wake up, goddamnit, what are you thinking of! I'm the one who needs sleep—and Humberto and Braulio and Luisa; we all need to sleep, and the crowd of early risers that had insulted and stoned them minutes before needed to sleep, too—sleep . . . sleep . . . turn yourself off . . . sleep like a log. Let somebody else take the wheel, the rudder, the ax, the hoe, the tractor. Sleep, you son of a bitch, what are you doing, why don't you wake up? Who are you to close your eyes?

"Wake up!"

He began to shake Gregorio. He opened the car door, jumped out, grabbed Gregorio's arm, and dragged him out. Gregorio half opened his eyes, trying to stay on his feet, while Julio heaped abuse on him like a madman. Leaning against the door, Gregorio looked uncomprehendingly at him. Julio picked up a chunk of dried mud and threw it against the car, making the metal hull clang. The pulverized earth spattered against Gregorio.

"Wake up, you son of a bitch. Nobody has any right to sleep here."

Gregorio picked up a chunk of dried mud, too, and threw it at Julio, but missed.

Staggering and lurching, like a prizefighter, his arms tense and his fists balled, Julio came toward him.

"You got dirt all over me!" Gregorio shouted. "Are you crazy? What the fuck is wrong with you? Who do you think you are?"

Julio roared with laughter. "I know, goddamnit. I'm Marx, Karl Marx, and you're nothing but a mouse on the margins of history."

"Well, I'm Engels, you old shit. I'm Engels, you hear!" Gregorio shouted back, and began to turn, carefully gauging his opponent's every move, guffawing. Gregorio and Julio crisscrossed, battling over and sharing the angry rocky ground of reality and fantasy. "Get ready, pussy. I'm Engels."

"An old fight." Julio's voice was hoarse and really angry now. "A true struggle of contraries. All your shitty dialectic, your desire to make nature into history, your four hundred proofs that aren't worth a slice of pickle, not even a pinch of opium."

"Show me, you theologist, always imitating Hegel, you wrinkly assed Prussian."

They howled, face to face, circling each other on the rocky ground.

"My whole life come to this!" Engels shouted.

"For you to be owl-bait!" Marx shouted.

But Engels leaped with such suppleness, such skill, that Marx mistook him for a four-winged bird with sharp, steely eyes and a huge beak, set to attack. And he flew square onto his shoulders, and Marx's head struck a rock among the mangroves, a few steps from that other body, fallen, too, in the charge.

It looked hopeless to Lucrecia. Caruca nodded. They were naked on the beach, all their old modesty set aside. Times changed and they changed with the times; but not their father—he refused to look at him laid out there, with that long, kinky, bloody hair and that beard with its white hairs—his own was not a bit grayer.

"If you had only left, if you had only taken my advice, but you were always the renegade, just like your father and grandfather." His mother looked paler, older. She came out of the waves, dragging the trunk; the great schooner moored to the cliffs swung on the water and hundreds of sailors disembarked. He could hear the droning of their conversation.

"What love for that trunk! What fucking love for that trunk!"

"You've cracked your skull. You're all bloody. Stand up and get 'im. Tear him up."

A few steps from him, his father vehemently scolded him. Tin came up limping a little, timidly wagging his tail. He sniffed; his flat nose sniffed his unmistakable smell, but his wide-open, sharp eyes didn't recognize him.

"Strange way to fall, exactly on that rock, exactly on the base of your skull, and all that blood they'll never be able to stanch."

He tried to obey his mother, more out of love than shame at finding himself fallen before the hordes of Russians, Czechs, Germans ("They must have heard the argument, or maybe there's another bunch of foreign technicians living around here") making a circle around the rocky ground that his blood was dying the color of dawn. The sun gave a coppery glow to the people morbidly waiting to see what would happen. All this century's curiosity, he thought, has been tinged by the same perverse concern. No one expected miracles or resurrections, only catastrophes, collapses. The tangled manes of hair of new people arriving harbored the same fetid smell as the mangroves. Tin came up slowly, and he stretched out his hand and petted his filthy head, his ear. Caruca and Lucrecia turned their heads away. "Poor thing, they haven't bathed you for ages." Tin licked his fingers, stepped closer to his chest, nuzzled him delicately; then he put his front paws on his right shoulder and began to lick the blood. Julio felt the strange lassitude of the caress, and a growing withdrawal.

Waves beat against the cliffs, the spray smashed up in the air, myriads of drops covered their shadowed faces, gleaming in the cool morning like a layer of sweat, and that warm porous tongue went on lapping his blood. It seemed to Julio the only possible image for pity. Every man's head is a running sore, he thought. No one can soothe it without being infected—except a dog. And he turned over, breathing so weakly that Tin's panting seemed the strong burning breath of the people surrounding him. Now, turned on his side, he saw the beach sharply etched before him—the rocky place, the mangroves, the rows of palm trees, the huge sun, the breaching schooner, Lucrecia, Caruca, his father, his grandfather, the Czechs and Russians, the branches that creaked and bent under the steps of the curious people that kept arriving. He made out Braulio and Humberto coming up . . .

"Perhaps now, perhaps Luisa . . . now," he groaned, and looked for her among them, among the legs of those who stopped, more and more of them, along the gravel road, along the green line of mangrove trees beyond the muddy line of the culvert, along the edge of the asphalt road; he was still breathing, prudently, slowly, conserving his strength, rolling back his eyes, to open them suddenly when he heard her come . . .

Afterword

I WAS LYING on one of those wooden boards hung from the wall by two thick chains, like those in medieval dungeons, in a narrow cell of the Department of Security of the State of Cuba, when I heard the big steel door creak open. A guard ordered me to stand. It must have been very early in the morning; there was no sound from the neighboring streets. I was surprised once again that the man was heavily armed, since at every door in that stronghold with its labyrinth of hallways there was a guard who challenged you and gave you permission to pass. I walked again the long stretch that separated me from the small, cold, overly bright office of Lieutenant Álvarez. I was his "case."

Each prisoner is always interrogated by the same officer. The socialist world's outstanding contribution to jurisprudence is that policeman, investigator, and examining judge are one and the same person. Perhaps they do it that way to speed up the work of the tribunals, whose only function is to hear the charges of the prosecution and deliver the sentence, without ever considering how the investigation might have been conducted or its conclusions arrived at. The defense lawyer merely pleads for clemency in the name of the generosity of the Revolution.

Before entering the office, I went once again through
the ceremony of abasement, simple and brief, to which
all political prisoners are submitted. The guard grabs
you by the bare shoulders (since the prison uniform is
a kind of sleeveless overall, the color of baby shit, given
you at random, so that one week it may swallow you up
and the next squeeze you like a straitjacket), shoves your
nose against the wall, and stands at attention before the
closed door. Then, pitching his voice in a guttural tone
he thinks of as martial, except that some speech defect
makes what he says incomprehensible, he exclaims:
"Tinint, priznr jacintf'r sere byndmi!"

The phrase, which he has memorized, is too pompous
for the national temper; the guard pauses for a split second and, almost choking, finishes: "Mission tletiminter."

Of course, if one is Cuban and has heard it often, he
may manage to decode the phrase as follows: "Lieutenant, the prisoner you sent for is here behind me.
Permission to let him enter."

From within is heard an imitation of Fidel Castro's
voice, since every Cuban policeman's aesthetic and emotional goal is at least to *sound* like Fidel. "Permission
granted, comrade. Have him come in."

The first time I was taken to his office, Álvarez was
wearing a dress uniform and he behaved with the ceremonial air he might have adopted to receive a captive
general after a long battle, but today he wore U.S. Army
fatigues. His fatigue jacket was held at the waist by an
imposing green belt, from which a no less imposing
pistol hung. I was afraid that something had happened,
since he seemed ready to go into combat. His silence

and angry look added to my uneasiness. Moreover, this time he didn't order me to sit down. He was standing before the desk flanked by the two chairs we always occupied. Behind him I saw the door, ajar for the first time, which had intrigued me from the beginning, through which could be heard the incessant pecking of several typewriters, doubtlessly making copies of recorded interrogations that would be submitted later to expert analysis.

"We've had Mesié Pier Golendorf, notorious enemy agent, here for a month. We know what you said about his detention: 'To convince me Pier is guilty, you have to show me proof of his guilt.' And who are you that we have to show you any proof?"

I remained silent, but Álvarez didn't stop. "We have in our possession all the notebooks you keep your 'literary notes' in—which are nothing but reports to the enemy. You don't believe me?"

I said that Golendorf was a member of the French Communist Party and a friend of Cuba.

"Like you, right?"

He shouted then and abruptly took the manuscript of my novel *Heroes Are Grazing in My Garden* out of a desk drawer. I recognized it immediately by the two thick, hard, plastic covers that Soviet export companies use for their catalogues and I used for bindings. It was unmistakable.

"We've found all your copies. You made more than they do for *Granma* magazine, except *Granma* spreads the ideas of the Revolution, and you spread CIA poison."

He stroked the shining covers and smiled as he looked toward the door. "Your wife should be here with you.

You two are cut from the same cloth. She says she has claustrophobia, so the doctor has diagnosed her as a hysteric."

I said she had nothing to do with what I said, did, or wrote, that she didn't have to suffer my fate, much less be held for no reason at all.

"Is that a challenge?"

I said no, but I knew what I was saying was wasted breath, they had certainly picked her up moments after me. And they had. A cold chill ran through my body when I heard her tense, anguished voice emerging from a tape recorder, refuting the accusations this very officer was throwing at her. What did she have to do with my poems, my novel, my opinions? Why had she been unjustly locked up in one of those cells? Truly, I could never have imagined that they would resort to such tactics, dictated by blind hatred. If my imprisonment for "conspiring against the state" was an outrageous hoax, her imprisonment—when they knew she suffered from a nervous condition—could only have been the result of "policy," the term they use for high-level decisions which, though unjust, are considered necessary. In fact, they were taking their revenge, two years afterwards, for not having been able to stop the Cuban National Union of Artists and Writers from unanimously awarding me the national poetry prize. The jury, made up of both Cubans and foreigners, insisted so strongly on its decision, in spite of political pressures, that my book *Out of Play (Fuera del Juego)* was published by the Writers Union itself, though reluctantly. My novel was said to be only an attempt to create a new international scandal. The title *Heroes Are Grazing in My Garden* infuriated them: only *animals* graze—

horses, for example, which was Fidel Castro's nickname in those days.

To get an idea of the paranoia with which State Security reads the work of Cuban writers, consider the case of Virgilio Piñera. He published his collected poems under the title *A Whole Life*, and included "The Horse's Path," originally published in the magazine *Silver Spur* in 1941. The police suppressed the poem at the last moment, even though Virgilio had shown them the collection. Ironically, "The Horse's Path" *did* appear in the index, since the efficiency of the police censors didn't reach that far.

I took the title of my novel from a brief poem by Roque Dalton, which begins and ends with the line "Heroes are grazing in my garden." Roque was a friend of many years, member of the Central Committee of the Communist Party of El Salvador, dead under circumstances that have never been completely clarified. He had a great sense of humor, of irreverence, and he was greatly amused that one of his lines might be used as a book title. But whenever the novel was mentioned in high-level gatherings of the police, the clever line was taken as an insult.

Well, there was no doubt now that vengeance and hatred could be converted into "policy," though I couldn't see the need to extend it to my family. There was a knot in my throat and tears came to my eyes. Álvarez looked at me condescendingly. "Cry if you want to; it's all right for a man to cry. But before you declare war on us you'd better ask yourself if you're ready for the bullets. You're intelligent, of course we recognize that. But we have to do something about this state of affairs with regard to the intellectuals of Cuba—

if we don't want to wind up like Czechoslovakia. In Czechoslovakia, intellectuals are all standard-bearers of Fascism, like that little Russian friend of yours Yevtushenko, who's anti-communist and anti-Soviet."

Yevtushenko had cabled me from Moscow, congratulating me on the prize awarded to *Fuera del Juego*. "It is a bitter book," he said, "but bitter truths are still truths."

I replied, though I was convinced it wouldn't do me any good, that history would be the judge. Álvarez shouted, "Counterrevolutionaries have no history!" I poured out my objections. I insisted that no one could ever prove that my wife and I were anybody's agents; I had sent the novel that was so irritating to everyone to the rector of the University of Havana, under whom I was working, so he could read it and give me his opinion; I had no intention in writing it other than to mirror some types and conflicts which emerge only in a revolutionary process: the very fact that we were being held in detention for a novel that had not yet even been published illustrated my point better than anything else. "You know that I've been to almost all the socialist countries," I said, "and worked in two of them. And in every one of them I saw very clearly that the political apparatus in the end becomes a force of unquestioning authority, political leadership unfailingly becomes alienated from its popular base. Instead of being here in a cell like criminals, my wife and I, I should be discussing my book at the Writers Union with my colleagues and the political leaders of my sector, not with the police."

"Yes, of course, over a cup of coffee and a good cigar, so you could then become president of the Union."

"You have a very bad opinion of writers, Lieutenant."

"Because they're all the same."

"All of them?"

"All," he said, "without exception. Did Che make exceptions when he said all writers are in a state of original sin?"

It was Raúl Castro's reasoning, too. Years before, in Prague, speaking to the Cuban diplomatic and commercial mission I was with, Raúl had referred to the controversy raging around Solzhenitsyn in the U.S.S.R. He had said, even then, "In Cuba, fortunately, there are very few intellectuals, and those there are do nothing but get bogged down belaboring the obvious."

The real motive behind an article entitled "The Provocations of Heberto Padilla" in *Olive Green* magazine was that the magazine, the official organ of the Cuban Armed Forces, was at that time publishing editorials which clearly implied that Raúl Castro was at last purging the cultural sector of the country. This was an old ambition of his; he had done it for the morals of the country when he created the infamous Military Units for Aid to Production (MUAP), forced-labor camps into which hundreds of homosexuals were crowded in Camagüey province. Both purges showed his style—coercion, repression, jail. I will never forget the impression of Raúl that Waldo Frank left me with in Havana in 1960: "There is some deep abnormality in Raúl. He's cold and cruel and might even be capable of crime." A Cuban writer who was with us gave me a terrified look. We were both frightened by that vision of Raúl, but we believed it was subjective. After all, Frank was an old man and in the habit of judging men and stories by his own brand of religious ethics.

"The moment will come," Álvarez went on, composed once again, "when every citizen will be a member of the Interior Ministry, as Fidel wants. Then no one will have to be detained. But today the Party has assigned us this job and we are doing it."

He took the novel and thumped it on his desk. "Do you know what the title of your novel ought to be? Can you guess?" He came to within a few steps of me. "The inconclusive novel, buddy, in which nothing happens, nothing *can* happen. A few pages read by a tight little group. But it'll wind up where it deserves, in the trash— because what good is something fragmentary, unfinished, incomplete? Fidel doesn't like this poisonous shit, the leaders don't like it, the Party, nobody likes it."

And he seized the manuscript with a fury I'd not witnessed until then. I didn't see or hear anything more. When I came to, I don't know how much later, I was no longer in his office. A huge weight seemed to press down on my head. Next to the board I was lying on, a doctor was taking my pulse, listening to my lungs and heart; then he left without a word. For a few moments I tried painfully to reconstruct the scene, but my head felt three times its size and all the blood rushed to it; my ears rang; it was a struggle to breathe. I managed to get up and went to the water tap, tucked into a corner of the minuscule lavatory, no more than a hole in the floor. I splashed cold water on my face, all over my head, and I pissed blood while my nose also bled.

A cold unusual for March filtered through the three chinks high on one of the walls, openings to the outside for air; the cell was filled with a kind of mist through which I could make out walls scribbled with the end of a spoon—poignant inscriptions, farewells to the world, scraps of prayer, which I forced myself to stop reading.

Afterword

There was a light bulb above the doorway, protected by a steel mesh. I heard voices coming down the hall they herded all of us political prisoners through when they led us to an interrogation. We never saw one another; to avoid that possibility, the guards used whistles to signal that some prisoner was being moved. Once, when I was about to run into another detainee, two whistle blasts sounded simultaneously and they pushed my nose into a wall until they could hide the other man and I could go on down the hall.

I felt terribly weak, terribly tired, and went back to the wooden board, but when I tried to get up on it, my strength failed me and I fell full-length on the floor of the cell. My feet must have knocked against the door, the noise must have been heard, I don't know; the light of a flashlight shone through the peephole. Then the door was opened.

I found myself in the Military Hospital at Marianao. The place was roomy, airy, and you could see trees through a high window. The nurse had finished taking my electrocardiogram. A man's booming voice filled the whole place. "I'm a friend of Ramirito Valdés and Sergio del Valle." And he went on adding names of political leaders to an inventory nobody was paying any attention to—the guards, doctors, and nurses carried on with their duties. In a while the iron grating of my room opened and a fairly young nurse came in—unattractive, but cheerful-looking—and put a thermometer under my arm, in the Cuban manner. I took advantage of the occasion to ask about the man; she would tell me only that he was under psychiatric observation.

"But if he's crazy, what's he doing here?"

"He's being treated—but of course his case is different from yours. I've read your books, we talked about them when we were young—your influence can be harmful to young people. But we have instructions to give you the best treatment we can in this hospital. I have orders to let you choose your own lunch and dinner."

She took the thermometer and looked at it with concern. I snatched it from her.

"That wasn't necessary," she said. "You have a fever of 104. I'll give you two aspirins to bring it down."

Now the man was jumbling together all sorts of political figures—those in the government and those in exile. He was a friend of Raúl Castro and Raúl Chibás, of Ramiro Valdés and Hubert Matos. It was maddening.

"He's crazy," I said to the nurse, and she turned before she left: "But he had his own explosives factory."

She came back with two aspirins, and in half an hour the fever began to subside. As it did, I felt a growing lassitude that brought me images of my wife locked up in a cell at State Security; of my children, who wouldn't have gone to school, to avoid questions and taunts from the teachers and the other children; of the friends who would be in danger because of my arrest—I had no doubt that this was the beginning of the iron-fist policy Raúl Castro had so strongly advocated, had so keenly desired to direct personally. Vitali Voroski, the first correspondent *Pravda* sent to Cuba, who used to visit Raúl often, said to me one day as we were walking along the Avenida del Puerto: "Be very careful of what you say—be very careful." He said it warily. Vitali had an intense nature, a sharp intelligence; he was a cultured man who had fought in World War II and was a mem-

ber of the Soviet Communist Party. Knowing what I
now know of such things, I have no doubt that he was
an agent of Soviet intelligence. That day he was accompanied by a young writer, whose name I don't want to
disclose now, but with whom I have more than once
discussed those words. Why did he warn us that way,
leading me to imagine the most terrifying possibilities?

He said to us: "*Pravda* has sent me word that in a few
days a young Russian poet, more or less your age—
Yevgeny Yevtushenko—will arrive in Cuba. I have not
met him, but his poems are published in *Pravda*, and
that means a lot in the U.S.S.R."

We didn't know the name either. Was Voroski trying
to warn us against Yevtushenko?

"The Cuban Communist Party is still Stalinist,"
Voroski added. "The newspaper *Today* has not even
published Khrushchev's speech to the 20th Congress, and
looks with some disfavor on Yevtushenko's trip. They
say the anti-Stalinists of today are the anti-communists
of tomorrow. It horrifies them that Yevtushenko might
become friends with any of the young comrades from
Revolution Monday." *Lunes de la Revolución* was
Cuba's most influential literary magazine, and apparently Fidel Castro didn't want Cuba's young literary
talent "corrupted" by Yevtushenko.

Vitali paused, adding in a low voice: "Listen to this
and listen carefully. Enemy number one to all of you is
Raúl, and one of his biggest phobias is culture in
general. They say the only thing cultural whose existence he recognizes is the waltz."

This iron-fist policy knew no scruples. The first signals
came from *Olive Green* magazine—defamation, insults.
Why did Fidel Castro tolerate, or perhaps back it? We

Cuban writers were not unconscious of the hostility with which foreign intellectuals, who almost unanimously defended the Cuban Revolution, reacted to the revolutionary government's support of the Soviet invasion of Czechoslovakia, even though, after that first statement, the Cuban press published the broadest, most objective version of the facts—which led one to assume fairly certainly that Cuba condemned the invasion. Fidel Castro himself, in the speech in which he admitted the "bitter necessity" of approving the invasion, noted that his words would let a lot of people down. If he accepted this, why his fury at the international condemnation of his behavior, why take it out on us? We weren't even permitted Yevtushenko's luxury; he condemned the invasion from abroad during one of his many literary tours, and he hadn't suffered the least repercussion when he returned to Moscow. Was this a symbolic act—was knocking me around and throwing my wife and me in prison a way, in morbid reflection, of subjecting Jean-Paul Sartre and Simone de Beauvoir to the same harsh treatment? It wouldn't surprise me: Fidel Castro has been obsessed all his life with the thought of doing away with all distinctions of worth and superiority. He equates himself with Lenin, casts me as a tropical Sartre, and turns Cuba into the whole African continent. The political weight of a country makes the international stature of its leaders, its artists, even its critics and deserters. Che Guevara himself told me that, in so many words—at meetings of the Steering Committee of the Ministry of Foreign Trade, which on Thursday midnights would be down to its chief, the minister Alberto Mora, and me. Our conversations were always about philosophy and literature: "This boom of

Latin American writers is a result of the Cuban Revolution. Without the Revolution, those guys would be just a bunch of assholes running around Paris."

Standing up to a perfectly orchestrated, unscrupulous maneuver is utterly futile. There is no courage more impotent and unrecognized than a Cuban's as he tries to shout his truths at a police squad armed to the teeth. Your friends will tell you not to get stirred up; they know how much a petty official can count on to provoke you, and how much a victim has to lose. The only weapon against a bully is intelligence, cunning. Before bullies, it's not a question of balls. The Chief of State's balls are beautifully protected by a repressive apparatus, whereas a jailed writer's are highly vulnerable to blows and torture. "The Spanish shout, 'I swear it, by my balls!' Well, a bull's are bigger yet, and they cut 'em off," Galán, an old Asturian who loved the British crown, would declare. "England" was to him a symbol of all the world's wisdom. "Viva England!" he would cry in a stifling Cuban beer hall where piss couldn't have been a more horrible color than the stream of beer they poured for a peso into whatever was handy (there were no beer mugs), nor could beer have smelled more like piss. The old man got on the nerves of my friends Hubert Martínez Llerena and Alberto Martínez Herrera, but all three of us felt the menacing knife.

So Security was right from the beginning—the title of these pages should be *An Inconclusive Novel.* And everything that happened to me in Cuba was so grotesque and paradoxical that when I tried to redo the lost chapters of my novel I inevitably went back to my own experiences. The fates of these characters, as well as the situations they are involved in, are inconclusive, because everything written in a suffocating political atmosphere is inconclusive and fragmentary. In such a world, the pages of a book must be hidden, and "the absolute time of literature" that critics speak of, out of which they claim quality of genius comes, becomes secondary. What counts is the furious weight of the *message*. Books written under socialism are generally imperfect; the country's reigning, or for that matter clandestine, aesthetics stamps books with a feeling of desperation or neurosis. They are accepted abroad out of solidarity, rather than literary recognition; they are adopted books —adopted for the scandal they cause.

I was living in New York when the furor over Boris Pasternak's novel broke out. I can never forget the face like an angry hawk's that was displayed in all the bookshops of New York. I read the novel then, like many of my friends, with no heed to its other values. Years later, traveling and living in various socialist countries, I saw how people in those countries were reading the book, which circulated clandestinely among them. They read it with bated breath, heart throbbing, tears in their eyes. In Spain, the avant-garde publisher Carlos Barral, praising Pasternak's poetry, called the novel "mediocre and disproportionately famous." And the novelist Juan Goytisolo wrote: "To make a judgment about the novelty and importance of these writers, we consider only their thematic audacity, without taking into account, as in the case of *Dr. Zhivago*, for example, or Solzhenitsyn's novels, that in structure, order, syntax, almost unvaryingly they repeat the narrative ploys of the nineteenth century—a world pre-dating Marx, Freud, Ferdinand de Saussure," because, according to Goytisolo, "in countries with freedom of expression, there are no longer, as we all know, any provocative themes."

The Joke, by Milan Kundera, was published in London in 1965, I believe, due to the scandal that its publication caused in Czechoslovakia, but its editor restructured it to make it "accessible" to the English public. I remember the letter Kundera wrote to *The Times* asking people not to read that version, which was barely his at all. The defects in Solzhenitsyn's novels are often excused because of the urgency with which he wrote. Few people point out that those books require an impossible reading by an impossible reader, since no reader will have the kind of knowledge required for their understanding. It's a kind of writing for the blind.

This novel was saved by a miracle. Five copies of the manuscript had been discovered, but the original remained untouched in a wicker basket, among toys and bric-a-brac. The policeman's hand was suspended in mid-air—just as in a detective novel—when his superior, satisfied with the plunder so far uncovered, ordered an end to the inspection.

When Fidel Castro let me know that I had been authorized to leave Cuba, I took the manuscript and put it in a nylon bag among hundreds of letters my wife had sent me from the United States during the year we were separated. I showed the bag to Gustavo Castañeda, who had charge of me, and who had done all the paperwork for my exit. I told him I wanted to keep these letters with me. Of all the people who saw me off at the airport, only my friend Alberto Martínez Herrera knew the manuscript was hidden among the letters. He was tense and pale, and every second we had to wait made him more and more anxious. The plane for Montreal was unusually late, so that I paced the waiting room endlessly under the watchful eye of the Security officer dressed in his blue safari jacket that only clumsily concealed a pistol. I had the impression that he was looking at the bag with marked interest; but Fidel Castro had given orders to let me go. What would he gain by searching it? The news of the authorization for my departure had been broadcast internationally. Jan Kalicki, Senator Kennedy's foreign affairs adviser, was waiting for me that night in Montreal; the novelist Gabriel García Márquez had traveled to Havana expressly to interview me before I left.

Wanting to ease the tension of the wait, I remarked on the items the tourists—mostly French-speaking Canadian girls—were buying. I saw the rum bottles lined up for sale, and I told Gustavo I was going to buy one, but the cashier said they could be bought only with dollars. The Security man turned pale. He said he was going to the washroom, and when he came back, he offered to buy me a beer. Minutes afterwards, from a corner of the waiting room, someone signaled him. I pretended I hadn't seen; I went to the washroom myself. The plane was to leave in a few minutes, and I would be the first person on board, I had been told. The Security man led me through a side door and we walked across the strip toward the boarding steps. I saw a man approaching with a package; it was a bottle of rum.

"Our gift to you. Send us a picture when you drink a toast in the United States," the officer said to me. "No hard feelings, I hope." The fat, pink-cheeked, clean-shaven young man was smiling, as though he were seeing off a high official on a daring mission.

I have no hard feelings. Castañeda was my natural enemy, he had orders to be just that—to dog my steps, to inform himself of my opinions, to make veiled threats over the telephone whenever a foreign visitor expressed an interest in seeing me. Now his impassivity whenever I shouted angrily at him seems to me admirable. He never lost his composure, not even when he tried to prevent Gabriel García Márquez from interviewing me, a year earlier, in the Havana Riviera Hotel. I saw him approaching with two policemen posing as tourists, and I turned to García Márquez and said, "Gabriel, this is a State Security officer and two of his agents. He's come to keep me from asking you to help me leave Cuba. His name is Gustavo Castañeda." And Gustavo offered his hand to García Márquez—he didn't try to hide his profession, and he ordered his agents away.

He was a short man with a pale complexion, lank blond hair, and light eyes. Sometimes he was quite heavy and sometimes quite thin, depending on the ups and downs of his kidney disease; the last time I saw him he was in deep suffering. He had been divorced and was trying to make a more pleasant life for two little girls, his child and his new wife's. His brother had committed suicide in his office in the Philosophy Department of the university, where he worked. But Gustavo loved his job, felt enormous pride in it, and the truly great misery of his life was not being able to show off, at the Ministry of Culture or the Writers Union, where he was always hanging out, the major's uniform which was his glory.

I got on the plane and sat next to a window. I could see the airport I had freely passed through to go in and out of Cuba for many years, which one day was suddenly closed to me, on the decision of one man. Now, thirteen years later, that man had decided to open it for me again. The observation decks were full of people waving goodbye to those like me who had been set free—I saw it all with a sensation of unreality. Still standing a few yards from the plane, a few steps from the Canadian tourists walking up the steps, the Security officer contemplated the scene. I saw him for the first time not from a moral but from a physical height. He was physically, below, like the dead time of my anxieties.

My first encounter with Fidel Castro in my cell at the Military Hospital came back to me—the clamor of opening iron bars and the spectacular movement of the escort opening way in a place where even inanimate objects would have knelt to let them pass. I remembered him shouting at the guards—"Get out, all of you, and wait in the hall!"—at which his bodyguards faded away, and he waved a dossier, a shiny folder, and paced back and forth with great strides, but did not look me in the eye. "We two are the only ones who have to be here," he commanded. "Because today I have some time to talk to you, and I think you do, too; and we have a lot to talk about."

Yes, we had time to talk: time for him to talk his head off, to heap abuse on all the world's literature, because "getting revolutionaries to fight isn't the same as getting literary men to fight. In this country they've never done anything for the people, not last century, not this century. They're always jumping on history's bandwagon . . ." He must have seen himself as an impressive leader standing magnificently before a no less impressive adversary dressed in a faded uniform, a scar still bleeding on my forehead, my whole body aching from the kicks of this moment of history. Unforgettable encounter! I describe it in detail in my *Memoirs*, and I trust some-day he will write his version of this and all our other meetings, so we can both rest easy in our consciences.

I remembered the morning when I saw the most im-pressive face history can show any man. That man was me. It was about six in the morning, and Lieutenant Álvarez appeared with another officer, named Gutiérrez. They ordered the nurse to give me back the clothes I'd been wearing when I was arrested, and ordered me to get dressed. "We're going to the beach; you need a little air."

At that moment, the crazy inmate stirred in his bed and gave a long wail. His anguish-filled inventory would begin again now, name after name . . . The officers turned toward the voice, and the chief (Gutiérrez) made a comment, but I didn't get what he said.

We left and got into a car that was ordinary in every way except for a remote-control device that relayed its location to headquarters. At the end of Guanabo, in a heavy thicket opening onto a lovely solitary beach lit by the sunrise, we stopped. "Don't you feel better already?" Gutiérrez asked me. Álvarez sat on a boulder and he invited me to sit down too, but I refused, saying I pre-ferred to stand.

"Well, if you want to *keep* standing, you'd better think seriously about what you're doing. We can destroy you. We can destroy you even though you know that, legally, we have absolutely no reason to. You haven't done anything, haven't planted any bombs or committed sabotage or smuggled foreign currency. The Revolution will recognize all this in its own good time and we'll have no choice but to rehabilitate you—but today you represent a dangerous tendency in the country, and we have to eliminate that tendency. So there's only one thing for you to do—come around to our way of seeing things . . ."

We returned to the hospital cell in silence, and they left without another word. They had already said it all. The nurse came in, smiling as always, with a clean uniform for me. As she went out, she stopped for a second. "You'll feel calmer from now on, so you can think . . . That madman isn't here anymore. They've transferred him to Security. So you'll have peace and quiet."

And in the plane I thought again, too, of the poor, wretched man whose shouts I then began to miss, as the silence of solitude heightened my desolation. I was about to leave all that behind, down there, where the policeman was. I held on to my nylon bag, where my manuscript was; the plane's engines began to turn. At last we were rolling over the runway, and the officer disappeared from view. The plane took off, and I heard the stewardess's voice ask us not to smoke during take-off. The plane gained altitude and leveled off; I looked out the window at the great, brilliant expanse, that amalgam of greenness and luminosity that was my native land.